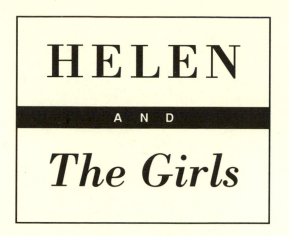

HELEN

AND

The Girls

Two Novellas by Hollis Summers

LOUISIANA STATE UNIVERSITY PRESS

Baton Rouge and London

First printing
01 00 99 98 97 96 95 94 93 92   5 4 3 2 1

Designer: Amanda McDonald Key
Typesetter: G & S Typesetters, Inc.
Printer and binder: Thomson–Shore, Inc.

Library of Congress Cataloging-in-Publication Data

Summers, Hollis Spurgeon, 1916–
    Helen, and, The girls : two novellas / by Hollis Summers.
        p.   cm.
    ISBN 0-8071-1757-9 (alk. paper)
    I. Summers, Hollis Spurgeon, 1916–   The girls. II. Title.
PS3537.U72H45   1992
813'.54—dc20   92-2870
                                                   CIP

A portion of *The Girls* appeared as the story "Diving"
in Hollis Summers, *Standing Room* (Baton Rouge:
Louisiana State University Press, 1984).

Publication of this book has been supported by a
grant from the National Endowment for the Arts in
Washington, D.C., a federal agency.

The paper in this book meets the guidelines for
permanence and durability of the Committee on
Production Guidelines for Book Longevity of the
Council on Library Resources. ∞

CONTENTS

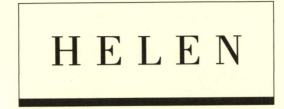

HELEN

I type easily.

I type in my cabin by a lake.

Even at the office I sometimes type my own letters.

The secretaries are named Janice and Mrs. Sowle. They are old ladies. They worked for my father. I will not mention them again. The world is full of people you do not mention again.

That would be a way to begin a log, a journal, a story.

I wrote suicide notes when I was young. I fancied myself as a writer. My father gave me a typewriter for my twelfth birthday. It was a green Underwood. I loved that typewriter. I wrote suicide notes and love letters to audiences: my father, actresses, the housekeeper—it was Mrs. Phalp when I was twelve—all the ladies on my paper route who asked me in to drink a glass of ice water. I tore the letters up. I burned them in ashtrays or I flushed them down the toilet. I assume everybody has imagined suicide letters: You will be sorry when I am dead.

This typewriter is a Royal. Anita gave it to me for Christmas. It has my name on the dust cover, embroidered. Anita is imaginative.

That would be another way to begin a story.

Ernie is a good guy. Ask a dozen people on Court Street about Ernie Hill. Over half, maybe all the people will say, "Ernie is a good guy." Ernie is one word: good guy, goodguy.

I am not particularly a goodguy. Other men on Court Street are described as good men, admirable, fine fellows, assets to the community. We talk easily on Court Street. I am those words.

You trust Ernie when you know he is lying. Or you distrust him when you know he is telling the truth. That is what goodguy means. I am not writing about Ernie any more than I am writing about Janice or Mrs. Sowle. Ernie is seven years younger than I am. For all practical purposes he runs Ben Adams Enterprises. I couldn't get along without Ernie Hill.

"Married virgins, they're the best kind." That is the kind of thing Ernie likes to say.

I wish I could talk the way Ernie talks.

Ernie and Anita, my wife, fly together tomorrow. They fly in a helicopter, scattering ashes over central Kentucky. The ashes belong to somebody named Aunt Della, Anita's aunt on her mother's side. I have talked to Anita on the telephone. She located me here at the cabin.

Anita was quite controlled, even almost jolly.

I said, "I'm coming to Kentucky. I'll drive down. I can be on the road in half an hour. I'm insisting."

"I'm insisting." Anita can insist harder than anybody. "I told you. Ernie's here. Let me do this my way. I know I've imposed on you. I know how you feel, felt, about Aunt Della. She was terribly difficult. I'll feel good if you don't come. You want me to feel good, as good as possible. It's all worked out. It's all splendid. There's absolutely no reason in the wide green world for you to be here."

I wanted to be loyal to Anita. I wanted to be particularly loyal. "I insist," I said, knowing I was not insisting.

"Please. And how did you leave Helen? I'm so glad you had your holiday."

We could have been people who shared a birthday, wishing each other happy birthday.

Anita said, "I just talked to her. I was disappointed you had left.

You must have had miserable weather. You should have stayed, another day or two at least."

Anita and Ernie will be home the day after tomorrow. Everything is working out. "You mustn't give it another thought. Promise, Ben. Promise me."

I love this cabin.

That would be another way for a man with a typewriter in a cabin at Lake Burr Oak to start a story.

We have a good life. We say so, everybody says so; we and everybody mean what we say.

That is another way to begin.

Sometimes, often, Anita says we are a family in a situation comedy, a series, and she is right. There is nothing wrong with a television family. There is nothing wrong with sociology. I do not watch television a great deal, but I have seen, at one time or another, most of the families at their weekly cavortings. The girls, Tina and Margot, have their favorite programs. I have watched a number of the shows from beginning to end, sitting with the twins in "the house downstairs." Anita likes to refer to our house downstairs. Often Anita watches with us; she knits or crochets, or writes notes, or pastes sequins on papier-mâchéd wine bottles for a church bazaar; Anita's work is seasonal; Anita never rests. The girls always rest, eating, swilling diet colas, laughing, often slapping their large thighs at the humor of the television situations.

"Isn't that hilarious, Daddy?" the twins ask.

"Yeah. That's great."

"Why aren't you laughing?"

"I am laughing. Look at my laughing teeth."

The girls find me humorous. Sometimes they choke at my retorts, spraying the room with potato-chip and cookie confetti.

And our lives are varied enough, set in sufficiently different scenes, among sufficiently mottled relatives, friends, and acquaintances, to make at least a full half hour's comic unit at least once a week, perhaps once a day. Anita, the Mother, insists on engaging in her charitable activities: Red Cross, the Hospital Guild, Care Line—where she answers a telephone and listens to problems about sex and alcohol and children. "I work half time," Anita says. "Half time means time and a half." Mother Anita says: "And I love every minute of it. I wouldn't change my life for anything."

The mercurial twins have relished their sophomore year at Athens High School, a year of laughter and tears, a year of bubbled excitement, a beautiful year. Anita says *beautiful* easily. The girls are beautiful, we have a beautiful life, a steak or a hot dog is beautiful. Not long ago I said, "I wish you wouldn't still use the word *beautiful*."

"Still?"

"It sounds so old-fashioned."

"Well, ex*cuse me*. I would hate to offend your delicate modern ears."

The little scene wasn't anything. I said, "Come on, Anita. I'm just talking."

She put her arms around me. "You're beautiful."

"I had a hard day at the office."

"Of course you did. Mmmmmmmmm." She kissed me loudly. The girls snickered.

I accept my father's monies. I have a tidy mind for money. With money no problem, a man finds other problems. I walk a tightrope. I suppose every man walks a tightrope between sanity and desperation, or perhaps desperation is a kind of sanity.

The girls are cheerleaders. Athens High School used to boast six cheerleaders. Now there are two, Tina and Margot, impossibly large, impossibly immaculate in their pleated skirts that barely cover their groins. "Give me a *A*," they shout, and all of the county responds. "Give me a *T*. A *H*, a *E*."

"Why don't you say *an* before the vowels at least?" I have asked the girls.

"Oh, Daddy! Really!"

Anita sits close against me at the basketball and football games. She has tears in her eyes, but she gives the girls a *A*, a *T*, a *H*, a *E*, a *N*, a *S*. I mouth the letters. I have never said them aloud. "*O, H, I, O.*" Anita shouts.

I, Father Ben, am the president of Benjamin Adams Enterprises. Ben is an interested citizen. Long ago, with his young wife's urging, he used to give six-minute talks to service clubs, 4-H groups, the high school. Ben Adams composed easily. "Six minutes is long enough," Ben Adams said. Sometimes he paused after he finished. Sometimes he said, "And on the seventh minute he rested."

He made the speeches from easy trinities. You can make a speech from anything. "You got to me, Ben," people said. "Those three *M*'s, I'll never forget them."

Ben Adams is ashamed of what all he can remember.

I've been through the alphabet, even the *X*'s, the *Z*'s—I forced them. Anita read and clipped. I made up the headings. Anybody can make up words for initials. I made up the words, Anita filled in the sentences.

Even this year I was asked to address the Rainbow Girls.

I gave up the speeches a long time ago.

I write book reviews for the Columbus *Dispatch*.

I will soon be, with luck, forty-five years old.

I've had an affair. Give me a *A*: Authority, Awe, Action. Give me a *F*: Freedom, Friendship, Fulfillment. Give me another *F*. Any issue of the *Reader's Digest* is full enough of illustrations to spell *affair*.

Father Ben relishes the pompous name of Benjamin Adams Enterprises no more than he relishes his rather artsy suite of offices over the Athens County Bank. Two years ago Anita found time to supervise the redecoration of all the rooms. She played among ten shades of green and blue; she bought paintings and art objects from the university's professors and students; all of the furnishings came from local stores. The relationship between Adams Enterprises and the community is excellent.

When Ben Adams got his first typewriter he told his father, "We are the Adamses. When I have children they will be named John and Abigail."

His father slapped him. "Adams is a name like Smith or Brown."

7

Anita's aunt Della always bragged about her age. "You wouldn't believe I was seventy years young, or eighty years young, or eighty-five." Ben hated her for bragging about her age.

Or perhaps Ben relished the Enterprises, while feeling the necessity of making fun of his good luck. He likes his handsome offices. Ben Adams' father, Benjamin III, was probably an unplated son of a bitch, but he was an efficient son of a bitch. He was a shyster, an opportunist; he was accepted, finally, because he made money. He had a big funeral with testimonies. Young Ben married Anita Vimont, didn't he?

Young Ben, twenty-five years old, sat in the church with tears on his face.

Young Ben, the remaining Ben, has never used a roman numeral after his name. Anita has said that not rearing a son is the one real disappointment of her life. Anita and Ben produced a stillborn son, before the birth of the twins. Girl twins run in the Vimont family. Anita regrets not having someone to carry on the numerals, but she has long since given up brooding over her situation. Anita, at thirty-nine, takes the pill. Anita says life is too beautiful for brooding.

Ben the Fourth had sense enough to amalgamate his father's interests: moneylending, water-softener tanks, real estate, a pizza parlor, insurance. Presently Ben, a relatively young man, leads an easy life. Ben, reared to talk poor, admits to himself that he leads an easy life. The Adamses spent two months abroad last year, and the firm showed its greatest profit in five years. Tina and Margot were bored with Europe. Ben is lucky to have Ernie Hill as his assistant. Perhaps Ernie, open, vulgar, loud, is a better businessman than Ben, a better cocksman. Anita Adams depends on Ernie, too. He makes out the Adamses' income tax and he remembers their anniversaries, and the twins often call him "Unc." He sends two dozen roses for everybody's birthday, even Ben's.

Anita, a goodguy, would naturally be attracted to a goodguy. "Whatever would we do without Ernie?" Anita says and says.

I think, honestly, generally, I think he is asexual. I can imagine being his father.

8

I like the sight of my name, Benjamin Adams, on stationery, office doors, advertisements, occasional little articles in trade magazines written by students at the Journalism School. We are very involved with the university. I like to work.

I like not to work when I choose.

I wish I were named John Adams.

I think I am not a vain man, I am not so considered. I remember to tell myself I am fortunate, financially, physically, most of the adverbs. Ernie weighs twenty pounds more than I do; he is three inches shorter; he balds, wearing his hair long to comb sideways and backward over his baldness.

Should I forget I am fortunate, and of course I forget, Anita reminds me: "We are blessed. Oh, Ben, we are blessed, blessed, blessed."

I agree. I agree.

"It's important to share our blessings," Anita says. "You agree, Ben. I'm not neglecting you. You're glad to have Aunt Barbara and Uncle Joe." Or the people we met in Nice, or the twins' friends from camp, dozens of the twins' friends, or a Cornell chum and her husband, or the cousins, or the single ladies, a lot of single ladies— Helen Cunningham, whom Anita met at a sorority convention at White Sulphur Springs back when the two of them were being loyal alumnae. Anita has never lost touch with anybody.

I have not minded. I have muttered on occasion. The lieutenant colonel husband of the Cornell chum was a violent Republican. The children of the cousin from Kansas were hardly to be borne. Aunt Della, may her ashes float peacefully, was never my favorite in-law; always Aunt Della told me that Anita did too much, as if her projects were my fault. "She's killing herself. You ought not to expect her to run a big house like this without full-time help. Full-time, Bennie."

No one else has ever called me Bennie.

Now Aunt Della has killed herself with being alive for eighty-six years. I do not pretend to grieve.

I imagine she has left Anita money. Anita is used to heiring.

We grow accustomed to monies.

Thanks to Aunt Della perhaps, some time ago Anita agreed to

have Mrs. Michaels come in four days a week. Anita is impossibly efficient. "But only four days. I can't bear the thought of having somebody underfoot *all* the time. I would absolutely suffocate."

And when the house promises to be intolerable, when the twins' guests from Miami and Middlebury appear simultaneously with aunts and the state diocesan woman's coordinator, there is always this cabin and The Book.

I like to think about this cabin. When my back gets tight and my neck hurts, at meetings, or over some rhubarb with Ernie at the office, whenever my easy world complicates, I can think about this cabin and think about a word like *peaceful*; I don't necessarily think *peace*, but *peaceful* is a good enough word to have hanging around in the back of your mind. The cabin is big enough for the four of us, but it has long bored the girls; Anita rarely finds time to make the trip. It is my cabin.

I can sit here on the back deck and disappear into the pine trees. In a while I will move to the front deck and watch the sun disappear into the lake. Tonight I will build a fire in the fireplace and lie on our vast bed, on the rough cloth of the coverlet Anita bought in Oaxaca. I will wait until I've turned out the lights to pull back the coverlet, to get between Anita's monogrammed sheets. *A. V. A.* the percale sheets say. Our lives are monogrammed.

I will look at the peaked ceiling that disappears and appears, even in daylight. I will think, perhaps, of cathedrals.

The Book started five years ago with Miss Averill's paper for the Friday Club. Miss Averill was the best friend of Anita's grandmother. Miss Averill's family entertained William the Conqueror, or William the Conqueror was her family: she had several versions. Her "Noble History of Court Street, Athens County, Athens, Ohio," was an utter fiasco. Even Anita's grandmother giggled during the reading. I liked Miss Averill. Never having known a grandparent, I am interested in people who can speak of generations. I can't blame Anita for my becoming Miss Averill's collaborator. I was truly interested in the material she had garbled. It was Anita who insisted that Miss Averill make a book of her information. I am not sure that Anita suggested I would help, but I ended up helping. The book,

Athens, Ohio, if you can call a pamphlet a book, is available at both the College Book Store and Logan's. Miss Averill insisted that the cover contain both our names. Anita gave an autograph party for us.

Miss Averill's last will and testament was as pathetic and gracious as she was. A full paragraph was given to complimenting me before she bequeathed her books and papers "with the ardent hope and faith that my young friend will continue his scholarly work under his own name." Anita and I attended the reading of the will at Charlie Jividen's office. Several people smiled at the reading, but Anita and I didn't. When we got home Anita cried. She said, "It's terrible to be an old lady," which is not the kind of thing Anita generally says. We made love that night. I remember that night particularly.

The New Book is a joke. When I have wanted to run out to the cabin for a visit, or even a weekend, I say, "I'm going to work on The New Book."

"You do that," Anita says. She protects me. I cannot imagine a more considerate wife than Anita.

Anita acts as if The Book were an actual project. Sometimes even I can imagine it. One could do worse than to consume himself with the men and women who have moved through the years of Athens County, a place that wanted to consider itself "the other Athens." This afternoon I read at one of Miss Averill's tattered reference books. I even got out her box of papers and letters. If a man let himself, he could probably manage to break his heart over Athens, Ohio. Miss Averill's notes, written in lavender ink, are almost decipherable. The box she left me is handsome: a single ivory rose blooms in the very center of the rosewood box; the latch is two clasped ivory hands; the surface of the box is unbelievably smooth; it is a sensuous experience to run your hands over. I suppose I pretend that Miss Averill is my family, going back to William the Conqueror. Anita was impressed when the old lady included me in her will.

We never became the other Athens. I do not expect us to, not any of us.

That would be another way to begin a story.

I write about Miss Averill to keep from writing about my own happy life.

11

I am a man of hobbies.

My father, or a school principal, or Mr. Hathaway at his grocery counter, or an auditorium speaker, maybe somebody at Harvard, somebody said, maybe I said it myself, "Distrust the man who has no hobbies."

"Sure I have a hobby," Ernie says. "Dog-and-cat is my hobby. I chase pussies." If Ernie says that one more time . . . I will listen to him one more time.

I have felt the necessity of hobbies.

When Anita and I married, I regularly played golf with a quiet man who worked at the university greenhouse. His wife, Terry, and Anita had gone to high school together. For a while Anita made her jokes about being a golf widow. "We widows should organize."

Anita and Terry learned to play golf. They joined us in foursomes.

Anita played better than I did. Anita has a knack for games. But her interest was short-lived. "Forgive me for doing so well that round," Anita said. "I shouldn't have done so well."

She found herself too busy for golf. "But you mustn't stop, Ben. And Uncle Joe adores golf. You must take him out. And Jean Shrader, she's coming next week. I don't think it's a silly way to spend time. It's marvelous exercise."

When we first built this cabin we bought a sailboat and an aluminum johnboat. I was a good Burr Oak sailor. Anita was very good. We sailed for a month. We fished for a month. "It's a pleasant way to sit out life, to enjoy life"—I forget how I explained it to myself. I enjoyed being alone, or quiet with somebody. There were two or three people I enjoyed fishing with, a young boy named Carlyle, a couple named Grean. Anita arranged expeditions for me. "Ben loves the water. He's going anyway. He has these marvelous boats. I'd love to go with you, but . . ."

After a while I stopped fishing.

I hunted for a while. Anita never joined me in hunting. "I can't bear the idea of those poor innocent birds and animals." I did not like the idea either. I gave up hunting.

12   I am not sure why rabbits and birds are essentially different from fish in the plan of God.

The dogs, Jack and Jill, named by the girls, were the joy of hunting. They were Llewellin setters. I hunted them only a few times. I lent them out. I knew hunting dogs should be hunted, I knew that much. Anita said: "They're beautiful, perfectly beautiful. But we won't let them in the house upstairs, maybe in the house downstairs, except for visits, short visits. I know Jack and Jill are becoming your best friends, Ben, but you'll have them altered. You wouldn't want puppies."

Jack and Jill lived on the far yard in houses almost replicas of our own. Anita had great fun designing the houses.

Anita expresses strong feeling against abortion in human beings. "It's Life, Ben!" She belongs to a committee of women who meet now and again. Only one of the women has more than three children.

Jill had one litter. I had Jill altered. I refused to have anything done to Jack.

I am fortunate to have Sam Dowkins in the tenant place over the hill. I see the dogs now and then. I do not think they recognize me.

One winter we skated at Dow Lake. We went skiing at Mansfield. It was a fine cold winter with a lot of snow. Everything looked like a Christmas card all that winter, but we did not keep going out.

One winter I made a banjo clock. It hangs in the den. One spring I bought old books. I went to several auctions with Jack Matthews and Bob Roe.

This cabin, the house upstairs, and the house downstairs, pay tribute to the wide and failing interests of the Ben Adamses.

I write about hobbies to keep from writing about my own happy life.

A dozen days ago Anita said, "Helen Cunningham will be here for a day or two. You don't have anything planned, not particularly. The Washington trip—that's on the weekend. You remember Helen. Big and pretty, the girl I met a long time ago. Stunning, really. She's been here before, maybe twice. You liked her. She's older than I am. Her mother died, finally died. That's terrible of me to say. I don't mean to be terrible, but Helen has devoted her life to her, her whole life."

It was after dinner. I was reading the newspaper at the counter in the kitchen. Often Anita says, "Keep me company," and often I sit in the kitchen; we make small talk at each other. Anita was loading the dishwasher.

13

I said, "You ought to let the girls do that."

Anita said, "I probably should. It's easier this way. And they're making tropical coats, for what tropics I can't imagine."

I said, "Helen was the one with the red hair?"

"Auburn. Well, yes, red. Pretty hair. I wrote her a sympathy note about her mother. I insisted she pay us a visit. She can't stay long. She's going to Ocean City, Cape Cod, one of those places. Her mother had a cottage. I read the letter fast."

I said, "I remember. She was handsome."

Anita said, "Genuine. She's genuine. She was a buyer when she was young. At Ayers, in Indianapolis, that's where she lives. They traveled a lot."

Tina or Margot called from the house downstairs. Often I can't tell their voices apart. Or from Anita's voice, for that matter. "Muth-er, Muth-err. The bobbin! The bobbin won't work, Muth-er. Can you hear me, Muth-errr?"

Anita rinsed her hands at the bar sink. She lifted her shoulders. She was smiling. "Muth-er. It's not the most beautiful word in the language." She leaned over and kissed me.

"You're tired, aren't you?" We often inquire of weariness.

"No, not really. It's just—they've been impossible today. I'm sorry I ever encouraged them to sew."

"You're patient with them. If they were mine . . ."

"They're yours." She kissed me again before she went downstairs.

I have never suspected Anita of faithlessness, adultery—whatever the word. It is natural for Anita and Ernie to be flying over Lexington, Kentucky, scattering ashes.

I assume a man suspects his wife to protect himself, to console, excuse himself. I wish Anita were having an affair.

I finished reading the paper. I don't remember anything else about the evening. I probably wouldn't remember Anita's mentioning Helen if the girls had managed their own bobbin.

14

We rarely argue over the girls, no real arguing. "We're *us* first," Anita has said. We have talked easily about the girls, through the Terrible Twos, the Tempestuous Fives, the Quarrelsome Twelves.

Anita has, I think, relished every age, finding comfort in the generalizing adjectives. "The Fractious Fifteens, we'll make it. Other people have made it. We're *us* first, Ben."

Anita loves the idea of challenge. So long as we can generalize about any situation, we are all right. And we can always generalize. I can imagine Anita's accepting death, her own, mine.

Helen was alone in the living room when I came home Tuesday evening. I put my jacket in the hall closet. I called, "Anybody home?"

Tuesday I came home and Helen was in the living room. She was big—tall, pretty, as Anita said she was. Her hair was auburn, piled on top of her head. She wore a yellow dress; the skirt was pleated. She was walking from the far end of the living room. She moved easily. She was extending her hand. "I'm Helen Cunningham."

I had forgotten about her visit. I said, "Of course you are. We've been looking forward to you."

We shook hands. "And you're the gracious host." She was laughing. "That's the way I remember you, gracious. I understand you've had company for the past three weekends. I don't see how you remember us all. Four years? Five? My mother was visiting friends in Nelsonville. I played hooky from Mother."

We were holding hands.

Normally I would have said something like, "Of course I would remember you." I have an easy tongue. I only smiled. Anita's right. Helen Cunningham is genuine. She would make a man feel silly for showing off an easy tongue. I did not mention her mother.

Helen said, "Anita's gone to pick up the girls at the country club. She insisted I take a bath and rest. She should have done the resting. I got here around three, and Anita has already managed several miracles. Dinner's ready, for instance."

"Anita has great faith in the therapeutic power of a bath."

"So do I. And if the painter calls, he's to be told firmly, 'Yes, we're expecting you bright and early Monday morning.' There's some complication about a Deedee's car, and Tina has lost a contact lens. And if you get home first, I'm to entertain you."

I said, "I'll entertain you. I'll fix us a drink."

She said, "Bourbon on ice." Generally, Anita's visiting ladies

15

take awhile to make up their minds. They ask what we are offering; they ask what we are going to drink; they often make explanations about their diets. They often say, "Oh, a little vodka, not too much, and a Coca Cola or Seven-Up; do you have Diet Seven-Up?"

Helen said, "And after the first, I'll have another, and not any more." I said, "I like for a lady to know her own mind."

When I got the drinks I forgot the napkins. Perhaps Helen's composure rattled me. I went back to the kitchen for the napkins. I said, "I'm being slow, I'm sorry."

She said, "I'd almost forgot how lovely it is here. The views." She lifted her hands to the windows that run south and west.

We looked at the meadows and the trees and the little hills that hold the sky and land together.

It's hard to realize that Anita and I built the house over ten years ago. We built on one of the farms my father acquired through foreclosure. It has been a long time since I've worried about my father's business methods. "You mustn't be silly, Ben," Anita used to say. "You're an honest businessman, that's what's important."

Indeed, for all practical purposes, I have been a righteous man.

I said to Helen Cunningham, "Yes, the views are good. A lot of days, seasons, I forget to look at them."

Helen said, "This minute is June, isn't it? Months are almost never the way I imagine them, but this is really June."

I said, "Of course June can be filthy when it wants to be."

Helen took a swallow of her drink. We were quiet.

I said, "I'm sorry. I forget what season you were here before."

She said, "It was fall. Beautiful leaves. There were three of us. We were being loyal sorority girls then—one of Anita's college friends and another stray, a librarian. They were terribly pleasant girls—women. We gave up our sorority loyalty right after that. That's funny to think about."

"Anita's still proud when the sorority makes homecoming queen or best averages, something like that. We have some of the girls to dinner, daughters of friends. Anita keeps terribly busy."

16   "I don't blame her—being proud, I mean. I would be proud, too. We hang on—we all hang on to what we belonged to."

"Oh, yes. The librarian had a dog, a Pekingese."

"Yes, yes. Named Doreen. I'm not making fun. And I'm selfish.

I'm glad to be alone here this time. However, I'm probably playing hob with your family life. But I'm glad to be here."

We were finishing our first drink when Anita and the girls came in, Deedee in tow. The girls were rather gracious; they both welcomed Helen; they both said, "Sure, we remember you." I wondered if they were telling the truth. Anita has trained them well.

Tina introduced Deedee. Deedee said, "I'm pleased to make your acquaintance," and burst into tears.

The twins began comforting her in loud voices, patting at her, offering Kleenex. "Poor, poor Deedee."

Deedee cried more vigorously. "My car, my poor car."

The three girls filled the room. I stepped back and knocked over the little table that held our glasses.

Anita, of the miracles, was herding the girls out of the room. "I know you're hungry," she was saying. "We won't be eating for a while. You'll fix what you want in the house downstairs. Hamburgers, french fries. Salad's ready up here. You're all right, Deedee. Everything's all right."

"Anita is . . ." Helen kneeled to pick up our glasses; she retrieved the ice cubes one at a time. She moved gracefully. I felt disloyal for thinking that Anita would have stooped over; Anita would have already finished tidying.

"Isn't she, though?" I was sure Helen was going to say *remarkable*. I hate to think how many times I have been reminded that Anita is remarkable.

Helen said, "A beautiful woman. I don't know anybody lovelier."

"Of course." A person gets used to Anita's being remarkable and lovely. I said, surprised at myself, "She's like the view."

Helen laughed. She made me feel pleasant.

I went to fix our drinks again, pouring Anita her little glass of sherry. Anita was back in no time. She sat on the couch beside Helen. Perhaps she was annoyed that we had not waited our drinks for her. Perhaps not. She said, "Let me tell you of my outing."

"Deedee had a wreck?"

"A flat tire. The Mobil man will fix it and bring the car here. But Deedee wants to spend the night. We'll put the girls in the house downstairs, if you don't mind, Helen. I'll move your things to the dogwood room, in the back, near us."

17

Helen said, "I like the idea of the dogwood room. Last time I was in the house downstairs." She was not making fun of anything. Anita says "the dogwood room," "the strawberry room," "the master bedroom" quite easily. Tina and Margot dwell in a suite named "Wedgewood."

Anita does not mind labels. She uses words like *upper middle class* and *liberal* and *intellectual* easily. Anita's mother and grandmothers referred to rooms by their wallpaper or motif; to people as well. Anita's customs inhabit our house. I am grateful.

I can hardly remember my mother. I imagine I can remember her saying she did not like Athens. But I probably do not remember. My father told me, "Your mother hated Ohio. She didn't want to leave Kentucky. She cried for three months." My father rarely mentioned my mother.

We had a good evening. Anita had suggested inviting Ernie for dinner. We often entertain Ernie, even when the single ladies are not present. I said, "Oh, I don't know," or something like that. "We've seen so much of him lately." I do not mind Anita's little machinations. She takes pleasure in arranging people.

Ernie will never marry anybody. "Why should I?" Ernie says, even to Anita.

Anita explained to Helen that we weren't having company that first evening because we didn't want to share her, a good time alone, just the three of us.

During the evening Helen mentioned her mother. Anita said, "I've been so grieved. She was so alive. So vital. She was a lady." Anita's eyes filled with tears.

Helen said, "I miss her terribly. I'm glad she's dead, however."

Anita said, "Why, Helen—you don't mean that. What a thing to say!"

"I'm glad to be able to say it. She was totally dependent on me. I was afraid I was so used to the dependence that I couldn't get along without it. I was the dependent."

"Did she suffer much, at the last?" Anita was whispering as if she were in church.

18

"Not at all. That was nice, too. She was having an argument with the maid, a violent argument. She just died. Of living. That morning she and I had had a violent argument. Over our next trip. Mama wanted to go around the world again. That was nice."

"My goodness, Helen," Anita whispered. "You don't mean that. Not that way."

Anita was trying to force words into Helen's mouth.

Helen lifted her hands. "I was the last of a breed, the professional daughter. I'm not sorry, not particularly—that I was a professional daughter, I mean, not that I'm the last."

"My goodness." Anita wiped at her eyes.

"Maybe I'll go back to work. I still know some people at Ayers. I loved buying, back then. It's even more exciting now; they send you everywhere now. I told you, I must have told you, about the first time I was sent to Paris. We were close then, the buyers. I suppose they still are, a kind of club. There was this funny, funny man from Chicago. He was terribly handsome, I thought so then."

I thought, "She is telling a funny story about a lover." I wondered if Anita knew. I watched Anita's face. Her eyes were as bright as if she had never cried. She was giggling.

"Helen, that is funny, funny, funny," Anita said.

We talked, they talked, about age. Normally Anita would have said, "I'm almost forty years old. And I don't feel a bit older than I did in my teens. Age is in your mind anyhow." Anita is considerate. She said only, "Age is in your mind."

Helen said, "Maybe. I hope so." I wondered idly how old she was. She sat in the white chair. The lamp, above her, lit her face. She looked young.

We talked about a book Helen and I had read, agreeing about it.

Anita talked about the twins, but not too much. Anita has been upset about drugs, and the stories the girls bring home. "But they tell me about it. I don't think they would tell me if . . . Ben thinks I fret too much. So many of the children sleep around. I could just die when I think about it."

Regularly Ernie boasts of the girls who have "given out" or "given in." I have listened carefully, pleased with his loose talk, the fine little details he includes in his narrative. I would never be able to tell anyone, even myself, the fine details.

I am an older generation. Thinking myself young, I know I am the older generation.

Helen, standing naked at a dormer window, looking at a motel, said, "I wish I ran a motel with see-through walls. I wish I were in charge of the whole motel. Life isn't long enough to be all the people you want to be—you need to be—I need to be."

It was raining.

Rain came in the open window where Helen stood.

I lay on the bed in which she had once been a young girl.

When she came back to the bed we did not make love. We had finished making love.

That would be a way to end a story.

In the upstairs house, against the pulsing tapes of the girls' downstairs, I said, "The girls are all right."

Helen said, "I'm sure they are."

Anita said, "You can't be sure. You can't be sure of anything. I know that. I've learned that much from motherhood."

I said, "Nobody's boasting. Every day is an act of faith."

Anita wrinkled her nose at me. She winked. I have long since stopped asking her to stop wrinkling, winking. "You like to say things like that. Ben likes to say things like that. You can see why people love to have him come to their parties."

I told her I probably did like to say things like that.

"Everything works out, I suppose, doesn't it?" Helen's sentences often end with question marks. Anita's sentences are statements. "I mean, I know. The cottage at Cape May, for instance? Mother dies; the real estate man writes that the place is empty, for the first time in ten years. He thinks I should sell. I'm thinking about it." Helen spread her hands. "It's good to have an excuse to go to Cape May in June. It can be lovely in June. And Mr. Kimberly, the real estate man, he's been absolutely splendid."

20

Anita said, "Ben's going to Washington. It's this weekend. It's one of those conference things. Ben could help you. He's awfully smart about real estate."

Helen said, "That's awfully nice. Mr. Kimberly has everything under control. He thinks this is a good time to sell."

I said, "I'm not sure I'm going to Washington. Anita made me be on the committee. But I'll be glad to make suggestions. I'm good at making suggestions."

For a half dozen days I have thought about chance. I do not like to believe in chance. When I was twelve, fourteen, my favorite poems were "Invictus" and "What Is So Rare as a Day in June?" I memorized the poems.

Chance means you sit in your own living room with your wife and her friend. The wife says something, and you say something, and the woman says something.

The woman says, "Of course I'd love to have company on the trip, to Washington at least."

Anita says, "I didn't *make* him be on the committee. It's an honor, and it's good to be public minded. Ben doesn't get out enough. I wish he hadn't given up the speeches. He enjoys the conference. It's something about 'Business and the Humanities.' It's a government something—they give out scads of money. He's just attended twice, but he came back delighted."

I said, "And they send you enough reports and prospectuses to balance the national budget. Humanists and businessmen like to think up fancy projects."

"Next to the cabin, Ben likes to go to the meetings in Washington best. That's true. I'm telling the truth."

Anita described the cabin, the difficulties we had had with the builder. "We'll go out there. Ben, too, if he can get away."

Often Anita speaks of me as if I were a third person. Anita began to remember her family's place in Maine.

Helen talked about the cottage at Cape May. "I loved that place. Mama and Papa built it when I was a freshman in high school. Papa died there. Mama refused to sell it, but she wouldn't go back. I tried to get her to. 'Now, Helen Ruth,' Mama said. I hated for her to call me Helen Ruth. 'Now, Helen Ruth, the past is the past.'" Helen shook her head. "Oh, dear."

Anita learned to ride a bicycle in Maine. Helen had her first date

21

at Cape May, "a nice boy, two heads shorter than I was; I was mortified walking beside him on the boardwalk; we had chocolate ice cream at the Nook."

Anita was reminded. . . .

I listened to the women. I was interested. I do not have houses to remember. I remember a series of little apartments made out of old houses, on State Street, on Congress, on Sunnyside—all of the apartments have melted into one apartment, as the cathedrals we've visited melt into one cathedral. I do not think of myself as having been deprived. Still, I suppose I have foolish reverence for our house and this cabin.

Today I own some apartments made from old houses. I have rearranged them often. I have found joy in making new compartments, apartments, changing a two-house flat to five efficiencies, three compartments to two, four into a family dwelling.

"You really should ride up together," Anita was saying. "You'll be company for each other. Ben could even go on to Cape May, it's no distance." Already Anita was an authority on Cape May, when a week ago she could not remember the name of the place. "He could help with arrangements. And he could miss a couple of the meetings. They meet all weekend; that's when humanists and businessmen are freer."

"Indeed," I said. "Businessmen are freer on weekends." The ladies laughed as if I were funny. Recently Ernie had had a girl from Chattanooga; she was Miss Something—Cotton or Paper or Goldenrod. The girl, according to Ernie, was mad for him. She couldn't do enough for him.

I did not imagine sleeping with Helen any more than I could have imagined sleeping with the housekeepers my father employed to make sure I studied and exercised and said my prayers.

I could have said, "It's a fine idea, but . . ." But something. Anita's projects are endless. She does not really domineer. A small suggestion can redirect her planning. She does not sulk. The plan could have taken any direction: the girls' going with Helen—"the girls need a beach"—or Ernie's going: "Ernie hasn't had a vacation forever. Ben keeps his nose to the grindstone; but, understand, Ernie likes the grindstone."

I am glad Ernie did not go with Helen.

I worked all day at the office on Tuesday and Wednesday and Thursday. I cleaned up some unimportant projects that had been hanging over me. I could list the projects. But I knew they were unimportant even at the time.

When I left at six on Thursday afternoon Ernie said, "I guess you're caught up to Labor Day." I told him, "Thanksgiving," and I was off for Washington. I was not annoyed with Ernie.

I said, "Good night, boss." We have a pattern of conversation.

Wednesday the ladies drove to Columbus for the girls' orthodontist date. Anita has beautiful teeth. I'm sorry the girls do not take after her. I wear six false teeth on an upper plate. But my stomach is flat, my hair heavy. I am counting my blessings. I am imagining myself dashing, worthy of a spectacular brief encounter.

We had Ernie and the Whans for dinner on Wednesday night. It was another good evening. In the driveway, while I was directing traffic, Ernie said, "Man, that Helen's something. She could jump in my sack any time of day or night."

I said, "Come on, Ernie."

Thursday the ladies went to the cabin. Even the girls insisted on going. They considered Helen "fantastic." Anita had three couples for dinner on Thursday night. Helen wore a long dress of thin black stuff, and gold loop earrings. Her visit was thoroughly pleasant for all of us.

"Helen shone," Anita said when we were in bed. "She absolutely shone. I love for a party to go so well."

After the company left, the girls had come upstairs to talk with us. We talked until almost one.

On a Mobil map Anita marked the route to Cape May with an orange felt pen. The girls teased her about her efficiency.

Helen said, "I've never had a more comfortable visit."

Anita said, "It *has* been good, absolutely satisfactory."

Helen said, "Sometimes, like now—I don't mean to be embarrassing—sometimes everything seems good. Life is long enough and whole and . . . good." She looked at her hands, "I'm embarrassing myself." Helen's hands are not young.

23

The twins yawned. They kissed us all around. Tina said, "If we aren't up before you leave, you have a good trip." Margot said, "We're glad you came, Helen. Good night, Daddy. I mean, good-bye and have a good trip."

Anita said, "We should all go to bed. You'll want to get an early start. I hate for this to be over."

Anita and Helen kissed. Helen and I touched cheeks, as we had done every night of her visit. I always touch cheeks with the visiting ladies.

Anita bathed while I packed. Despite what Anita says, I make enough trips to be used to packing: shaving things, pajamas, robe, extra suit and shoes. I remembered the folder of reports: the proposed projects are sometimes foolish, but I was voting for most of them.

"Be sure and put in your bathing trunks," Anita called, "just in case." I threw in the trunks. "And a big towel, just in case." I went to the linen closet in the bathroom and got a big towel.

Anita lay in the tub. She smiled up at me. Helen is right. Anita is a beautiful woman. She is too thin, but the years have been good to her body, good for her body. I told her so. I said I felt sorry for the twins for having a mother with such a beautiful body.

"Ben, the idea." She covered her breasts with a washcloth.

"Don't do that."

"I feel naked." She was giggling. She slipped the washcloth down over her body. She sat up slowly. I leaned over and kissed her.

"You're a lecher," she said. "Go on. Finish packing. I'll be out in a minute."

After my shower I stood in the doorway of our bedroom, drying. Anita said, "I wish you would go on to Cape May. You could do with an ocean. You look tired. You need to charge your batteries."

"I'm not tired. Look."

Anita smiled. "You're also an exhibitionist." She turned her head. "I wish I were going."

I do not know how to generalize about men and women. I cannot even generalize about Anita and me.

I said, "Do. You're the one who needs a rest. And the girls need to be left alone for a while."

Anita said she would absolutely love to go, but there was the

24

League meeting tomorrow, and she had promised to help with the summer bazaar—she hadn't helped at Christmas—and the girls were in their little recital: "It's not anything; you shouldn't feel guilty about not staying for it." Anita often tells me I should not feel guilty. And she couldn't leave the girls anyhow, not without planning. "And Aunt Della comes Saturday. I just forgot to tell you; I wasn't keeping it from you. I hope she won't be a bother. You don't really mind about Aunt Della. You just tease about Aunt Della."

And so Aunt Della is dead.

I am glad I am not attending her.

Anita and I made love. It was satisfactory. It is almost always satisfactory to have sex with Anita, although she doesn't like for me to refer to making love as having sex, although some mornings I can't remember if we have had sex the night before.

Afterward I said, "Do you suppose Helen is a virgin?"

Anita said, "I'd be ashamed. You're always thinking something like that about my friends." She was almost asleep.

"Ashamed to think of it, or ashamed to be a virgin?"

"Ben, you're the absolute limit. But thank you for being so nice to her. To Helen."

I said, "My pleasure."

I have assumed, recently, these days, that nobody is a virgin, or has ever been. Except for Anita and the girls—they are surely virgins. Anita talks too much; I read too much. I like to think the girls are virgins. I know I am illogical. Regularly they have dates with people named J. R. and Kenny.

Anita said, "I love you." She made kissing sounds. "I'll miss you. I'm glad you're going."

I said, "I love you, too."

After a while I went to sleep. I didn't have anything particular on my mind. A lot of nights I have trouble going to sleep. My mind keeps getting stuck with commonplace phrases. That night I kept thinking *going* and *to* and *sleep*. I imagine I am not unusual. Sleeping and waking are, I suppose, difficult for many men.

I wish I had somebody else in town, besides Ernie, to listen to.

25

I packed Helen's car. The trunk was already fairly full. Anita had insisted that Helen do her grocery shopping in Athens, even wine and bourbon. Anita does not approve of drinking, but she likes for people's larders to be filled. "You won't want to be bothered with shopping," Anita kept saying.

Helen had three empty suitcases for bringing back "household gods, if there are any household gods left."

I drove. Anita stood on the patio, waving and calling to us. "You're sure you have everything? Have a marvelous trip. Good-bye, good-bye."

"Good-bye, good-bye. And thank you. Thanks again." Helen blew kisses.

I honked. For twenty years I have been honking to Anita the five blasts of "Shave and a Haircut."

My mind said *good* and *bye*.

The first fifty miles were neither memorable nor unmemorable. Helen complimented the girls and Anita and our friends and our housing. I said her visit had certainly been a triumph. I complimented the car, a Plymouth four-door, which drove very easily. Helen said she liked it because there was headroom. "And I like four doors. I do a lot of chauffeuring. I used to." She said it was awfully nice of me to drive as far as Washington with her. "You could have taken a plane tomorrow morning, couldn't you? I'm just now realizing. I'm not very considerate." I said I hated taking early morning planes. Helen said she hated to travel alone, really.

I didn't think of anything much to say, so I stopped talking.

Occasionally Helen lifted her hand to a hill or a stream and said, "Pretty," or, "Nice." I was conscious of her perfume. She smelled like spring flowers. Anita wears a heavier perfume.

She lifted her hand to a red-winged blackbird that flew in front of us.

I said, "We have a lot of them. Is this too much air on you?"

"No. Just right."

Helen laughed. "I put on too much perfume this morning. Do you suppose I am trying to woo you?" She lowered her window.

"That would be pleasant." I was laughing too.

I thought about making conversation. I thought, "There isn't any need." I thought about the words, *there, isn't, need*. I thought about reaching over and touching her, patting her thigh—Anita and I often pat each other on a trip.

Traveling with Anita is a busy-ness. She peels fruit, she pours coffee from the thermos. When she isn't writing letters, she talks while she crochets.

I said, "We forgot the coffee thermos."

"And those marvelous cheese things. Anita had them ready for us. They were on the desk in the hall."

I was surprised that Anita had forgotten to give them to us. I said, "I'm not surprised I forgot them, though." I was only half listening to what we were saying.

The whole trip could have been that way—easy small talk, no talk, two friends shared the comfortable anonymity of an automobile, moving from here to there and leaving each other.

But at that long stoplight in Clairville, West Virginia, before the sharp turn at the end of town, I pulled up in the left lane beside an old Ford convertible. I nodded to the driver, a young man who wore his hair in a ponytail. The girl beside him wore huge pink curlers. Even the twins have never owned such vast and ugly curlers. The girl sat with her knees pulled up, almost to her chin. Her knees were large. Helen smiled at the couple and said, "Good morning." The young man did not speak; the girl said, "Hi."

Helen nodded to the girl's knees. "Twins?" Helen asked pleasantly.

The girl said, "Whut?"

"Twins?"

The girl put her legs down. "What's the matter with you, lady?"

Helen pressed her hands against her cheeks. "Oh, my goodness. I thought your twins were . . . I thought your knees were—Go on, Ben."

"The light won't change." I was trying not to laugh.

"I'm sorry. I'm terribly sorry," Helen said to the couple. "I thought—" Her shoulders were shaking. She couldn't hold her laughter.

"Smart shit," the young man said.

The light changed. I swung ahead of the convertible. "Fast, fast. Please, God. Oh, my heavens."

27

When I tell Anita about the minute in Clairville—should I tell Anita—she will say, "Helen thought the girl's knees were babies' heads. I guess you'd been talking about the girls, and Helen had twins on her mind. I can understand that."

But Helen and I laughed through Pennsylvania and Maryland. And we talked. We talked about everything, the way young people used to talk on dates, wanting the other person to know everything, wanting to learn everything.

Perhaps young people still talk such talk on dates. Perhaps Anita is wrong. Perhaps they do not spend all of their time having sex with each other. Perhaps they laugh together.

Once I pulled off the road at a rest stop to laugh. Helen had tears in her eyes, the only time I ever saw Helen's tears. She is not a witch incapable of crying. "And you heard what he called me. Oh, my heavens!"

I was sorry she had not brought herself to quote the young man. The words would have been hilarious in Helen's mouth. Anita would not have said the words either. I said, "Twins, lady? No, she has knees."

"Oh, Ben."

At lunch at a Howard Johnson's Helen said, "Last night I wondered what we would talk about. Isn't that funny? Sometimes I have trouble, with some people. Sometimes I resort to, 'Who is your favorite movie star, and what is your favorite color?'"

"I'll never believe that."

We were laughing again. The waitress came to our table. She said, "May I get you anything?"

Helen said, "Thank you, we have."

I had never heard a funnier sentence.

"We're too old to be acting this way." Helen was whispering. "Think about something very sad until we get out of here."

I couldn't think of anything sad.

28

We talked about being young, the pain of being young. We talked about movie stars and colors.

Once Helen took a truckload of Ayers clothes to the Cloister Hotel, at Sea Island. They had a cocktail show at four, a patio show at eight. "And I wore Ayers clothes all day. I wore them in Indianapolis, too. To the opera. I was an advertisement. Isn't that funny to think about, Ben?"

I told her it wasn't funny at all.

Once she ran a bridal clinic. "That's funnier still, Ben."

There was an accessory buyer. "I was in love with him, Ben. I was absolutely in love. Mama would have died at the idea."

I talked about my father. I spend very little time remembering my father. And the housekeepers we had in the funny apartments, and my going to Harvard—I rarely think about Harvard.

Helen talked about Oberlin, and the trips she had taken with her mother, and their living in Lisbon for a while; she did not mention her mother's death.

But chiefly I remember our laughing. Helen's laugh is easy. It begins in her throat. Her laughter is a communal act, like dancing. I did not think, "Helen's laughing," any more than I thought, "Helen breathes." We laughed together. We listened to each other.

Helen said, "Why am I talking so much? I'm a jabberbox. Mama always said I was a jabberbox."

I told her I enjoyed hearing about the mechanics of people's lives. "Like what do you do in the morning, and what in the afternoon, and where do you go after the plane lands?"

"I do too, Ben. Tell me."

I said, "You haven't jabberboxed at all. You haven't said a word. I was just thinking . . ."

"I want to know more about when you were fourteen. I want to know about your father, more. Isn't that a flirty thing to say? I don't mean to sound flirty."

I said, "It's not so terrible to be getting older. Not so very terrible."

"Not so very terrible to be . . . to be older." She did not name an age.

Once Helen said, "Would you mind stopping at the next rest room, bathroom?" I was glad she did not say powder room. Anita and the girls are very delicate.

Once Helen said, "Oh, dear."

"Oh, dear, what?"

"Oh, dear, it's been a pleasant day."

Road signs advertised Washington: hotels, motels, television stations, banks. There was a billboard for the Lewes–Cape May ferry. I said, "They leave at five and eight-thirty."

Helen said, "That's marvelous. You'll go to your hotel. I'll be early for the ferry. I'll eat at Rehoboth. I'll walk on the beach. When I was little we went to Rehoboth—before they built the Cape May place." Helen's voice was bright. "Who else but Anita would have thought about the groceries? I'm forever beholden to Anita."

It was raining. The traffic was heavy. I pulled out to pass a U-Haul truck. A car honked behind me.

Helen was talking about Rehoboth. Not once during the day had she said, "Careful," or, "Did you see that car, Ben?" or, "Slower, Ben, we want to enjoy the scenery."

I said, "There's no need for you to fight this traffic. I'll let me off up here a little way. I'll get a cab into town."

"You'll do nothing of the sort. I am probably the world's best driver in traffic. And I'm early. I'm so very early. And I love Washington. I'm always proud of Washington, D.C. I'm just like somebody out of the *Reader's Digest* about Washington."

I turned the windshield wipers to fast.

We were quiet again.

A station wagon passed us. A little girl with Shirley Temple curls pressed her face against the back window. She stuck her tongue out. Neither of us mentioned the little girl. A bus passed, and then a truck. The windshield was muddy water. For a moment there was no road in front of us.

In the living room at home Anita had said, "You'll take 270 and go in by Bethesda—that's what Ellin Quigley does—she's always going to Washington. Of course, you could go in by Chevy Chase or Silver Spring or College Park." Light caught the enamel of Anita's fingernail. Her long forefinger lighted the road. For a small woman her fingers are remarkably long. "Helen can get back to 495, 50, and 301 past Annapolis, to 404, the ferry, and you're there."

30

Helen cleared her throat.

"I think you missed the turn, Ben. That was Bethesda."

I did not answer.

"Here's Chevy Chase, Ben. Up here, the turn. Listen to me, Ben. Ben, you're—"

"I'm going with you." My voice sounded clotted. I cleared my throat. "I'm going on with you."

"No, Ben, please don't."

I was laughing. I was pretending to laugh. I said, "I don't want to go to those meetings. You can't imagine how dull they are. They say *input, output,* and *thrust,* that's all they say. We say the words over and over. They haggle over five hundred dollars and then they give a grant of fifty thousand without batting an eye. That's what's wrong with the government. They can't think little. It's important to think little. I'm telling you, Helen."

"Ben, please."

"It's not anything. I just want to see Cape May. I've never been to Cape May. We can probably make the five-o'clock ferry."

"I wish you wouldn't."

"Anita will be pleased. She said I needed an ocean. Anita is almost always right."

"Ben. Look. Look. All the roads lead to Washington."

"You don't want me to drive with you?"

"It's not that. It's . . . No. No, I don't."

"I'm going with you."

That was the way it was.

Helen said, "All right, Ben. Good. 'Good on you,' that's what they say in New Zealand. We had a marvelous time in New Zealand. The whole country seemed thirty years ago. Mama adored it. So did I. It was our last trip, already a year ago."

Helen said, "I went on the Cream Boat from Russell; it's a tourist attraction, but they still deliver newspapers and milk and packages. It was a day like this, scattered sun. Mama didn't feel up to going. There weren't many people on the boat. I spent the day talking to a young man from Los Angeles. I saw him just that day and the next. I felt I knew him better than anybody, even the people I've known all my life."

Helen said, "Excuse me. I'm making conversation. I don't mean to be making conversation. Don't let me make conversation. I hate that."

31

She held her hands back to back, palms out. I said, "You look as if you were ready to play 'Here's the church and here's the steeple.'"

"'Open the door, and here's the people.' Doors? Here is? Here are?"

She let her hands fall to her lap.

I reached for her hand. Her hand was cold. I did not take my eyes off the road. Perhaps she reached for my hand. We held hands for a minute, I suppose it was a minute, like children. One of us pulled away. Perhaps I did. Perhaps there was a sharp curve.

We moved across a landscape together. The landscape could have come from a nineteenth-century illustration for a children's book, a colored illustration. I have bought several such books for the girls. Hills rose beside us and in front of us. The color was not true: blue, or gray, or green, or brown.

Helen said, "The hills look as if they had been torn from construction paper."

I said, "Yes, exactly." Fog moved with the hills.

I would like to remember what I thought at the sign that said Bethesda, or the other signs that told people how to get to Washington, D.C. I would like to remember the "moment of decision" that preachers talk about. I would like to remember the way I used to think about myself.

I think I used to think Ben Adams, admitting the possibility of chance and catastrophe, lives an ordered life.

Every man lives in compartments.

Ben Adams admits the compartments.

What he does at a convention in Chicago has nothing to do with his wife and home.

I have said such things at parties. "You probably have something there, Ben," somebody says. "No, Ben, life itself is the compartment," somebody else says.

32

We sit virtuous and a little drunk at parties, telling each other we are contented.

I had no moment of decision. I merely did not take the exit. I would like to think I was impelled, that something stayed my hand.

I was sad. I was thinking of something sad, as Helen had told me to in the Howard Johnson's. But the something sad bore no name. Perhaps it was the reality of my compartments, or loving Anita, or not loving her, or being tired, or happy, or being regularly blessed, or being alive, or not enough alive, or dead.

Helen said, "I'm glad you're going with me. I'm not making conversation." She touched my arm. "Anita will be pleased. I'm pleased. You're pleased, aren't you, Ben?"

"I'm pleased."

I thought, "'I'm pleased,' said Ben in his jolliest voice." I was detached. If I felt anything among the hills and the fog I felt detachment—from both of us.

"And we can make the five-o'clock ferry. Hurry."

I hurried. I concentrated on the narrow road, held together by a yellow line and a berm.

Helen said, "Fifty miles an hour? That's too slow a speed limit. I'm furious with this state. What state are we in, anyhow?"

I said, "A state of euphoria," because I knew the answer would please Helen. She was pleased. We smiled at each other.

I thought, "You are old, Father Ben, to go a-courting." I thought, "You are young, Father Ben." I was pleased with myself. But I did not really imagine I was going courting.

"The ferry will be late, I promise you," the woman said. "Look, the rain's stopped."

The ferry was late. We saw it as we turned a curve.

"Hurry, hurry, Ben."

I was going seventy miles an hour into the toll lane. My wristwatch, an Omega, a present from the girls, said five-fifteen.

The ferry moved away.

"You missed it," the man at the tollbooth said. "You're lucky the cops didn't pick you up." He was a fat little man. His stomach stuck out over and under his belt. He was perspiring. I thought of my father. I thought, "Goddamn."

33

"It could have waited three more minutes," Helen said pleasantly to the man. Helen's voice is lovely. It is colored orange, or cream, whatever that means. Anita's voice is tan, light tan, whatever that means.

Helen speaks pleasantly to everybody. Even with strangers Helen sounds as if she were resuming a happy conversation.

The man said, "It's already late. And you're later."

"We'll be back," Helen said. "And thank you. Eight o'clock? That's right, isn't it?"

I thought of Anita, waving to us from the patio.

I said, "We missed the boat. We really missed the boat."

Helen said, "You don't have to sound desperate about it. We missed *that* boat, not *the*. I wanted to see Rehoboth anyhow, however."

And so we saw Rehoboth and environs.

We drove several miles down the beach to a place that was almost deserted—only an old man with a cane, a couple of boys chasing each other. I rolled up my trousers and Helen hiked the waistband of her skirt. Her suit was almost the color of the sky. Her legs are fine. Her ankles are thin, her calves firm. Helen Cunningham has long legs.

Ernie always says, "I'm an ass man, myself. Not a leg man or a tit man. I'm an ass man." I thought of Ernie. I was resenting him.

We walked barefoot down the beach.

I said, "Seeing the ocean makes you feel like somebody else."

Helen said, "I know, I know."

But I wasn't really seeing the ocean. The beach was narrow and cluttered. We had to be careful where we stepped. I tried to remember the way I have felt at other oceans. I wasn't listening to the ocean. I felt stupid in my tie and jacket, carrying my shoes and socks. I told Helen so. Helen laughed. "Poor old conventional male. I feel marvelous." I laughed a little.

I said, "I'm listening now."

Helen said, "I know," as if she knew what I was talking about. Perhaps she did. She took my arm.

We walked more easily.

The twins are nicer people at the beach than they are at home.

When we have approached an ocean they have said, "I'll see it first," and, "I'll hear it first." But they are not quarreling with each other.

"You heard it first; you saw it first," they have said to each other.

Helen and I had shrimp and wine at a little restaurant. We were early for the ferry; the ferry was late. We drank coffee and bought post-cards in the waiting room. There was the camaraderie of the drive.

I said, "Twins," and Helen spluttered into her coffee.

It was very cold on the top deck. I went down to the car and got Helen's raincoat out of the trunk. I realized I had not even brought a sweater. Who would expect to need a sweater in Washington in June, goddamn it? I do not think I spoke aloud, but I was afraid I had spoken aloud. I nodded to an old lady who sat in the car ahead of ours. She said, "Miserable, isn't it, though?"

We stayed on the top deck, leaning against the railing, until the hard rain started. We leaned against the fog. I thought of saying, "The fog is louder than the foghorn."

I am goddamned full of sayings. I was tired.

I'm sure we talked. I don't remember what we talked about. I did not even think: Helen and I will go to bed together. Perhaps I thought: Helen and Anita are great good friends; I am visiting Anita's great good friend.

Helen was shivering. I put my arm on her shoulders, the way a man puts his arm on a daughter's shoulders, or an aunt's by marriage. I did not take Helen into my arms.

I would like to remember myself as different. I would like to remember myself as Ernie, the way Ernie talks. I was probably frightened. I do not like to consider myself a man frightened of women. If I had tried to kiss Helen, sorority sister Helen, if she had pushed me away, if she had said, "What on earth? The very idea!" . . .

I was frightened. I was not considering Anita. I did not think of Anita. I would like to remember that I was considering Anita.

I said, "We have to get out of this. This rain."

We went into the little restaurant. We drank more coffee. We sat at a table with a young man from the University of West Virginia. He was working at a camp near Wildwood. "Yes ma'am," and "No

35

ma'am," he said, answering Helen's questions.

"I probably can't find my way around," Helen said. "It's been ten years. Can you imagine that? Ten years."

"I couldn't say for sure, ma'am, but I expect it's changed. I hear they've had hurricanes."

"Yes, yes. So I've heard." Helen's face was drawn tight. I wouldn't have recognized her if we had met suddenly in another room.

But I am always thinking that, about people's faces, away from familiar backgrounds.

When we went below deck the waiting old lady in the car ahead of us said, "Miserable." An old man sat beside her.

"Good evening," Helen said.

We were the fourth car off the boat. I followed the others. "Right? They're going right." I could see no signs.

"Right. Yes, I'm sure right is the way."

"And strait and narrow is the path."

"Oh, you did go to Sunday school, didn't you!"

"I am being funny. I am making up jokes. I never saw such a damn dark night."

"You are funny, Ben."

The old couple blinked for a left turn. Ahead of them the tail-lights of the other cars blinked right.

"Right? Right seems to have the majority." I turned on the car heater. I was not trembling, but I thought about trembling. I said, "I expect you're cold."

"A little. But good, all right. The heater."

I thought she was excusing me. I was annoyed.

It is no distance from the ferry to Cape May, but I imagined we were driving far miles. We went through towns whose houses held no lights. Trees arched over streets, making darker tunnels in the dark. I had lost the cars in front of us. "This doesn't look like beach country."

"I know, I know. Mama was always bragging. 'Cape May is green, not like Stone Harbour.' Mama was terribly proud of our lawn and the azaleas and hydrangeas."

"But this isn't Cape May."

"I know, I know. I'm not recognizing anything."

I heard her, but I said, "Talk louder. It's hard to hear you."

An Exxon station glimmered ahead of us. I said, "I'll stop and ask."

"No, we're all right. Turn right. I'm just being insecure and silly." Her voice was soft. "I remember the place as big and charming and the days long."

"Your mother said, 'The past is past, Helen Ruth.' That's what you said the other night. Last night. One of those nights. I'm making up jokes again." I leaned forward, hoping for the road. My forehead touched the windshield.

"I'm such a darn fool. I keep protecting the past. I keep wanting to tell the past, 'It's all right, Past, don't you worry. You were all right. You'll be all right.'"

"I expect I'm more like your mother." I was not wanting to remember any past.

"You're right. Mother was right. But she was always saying, 'The house will be full of children. You'll meet your husband in Cape May.' And I didn't meet a husband, and I didn't have children. Mama didn't worry at all. 'The past is past,' Mama said over and over. Mama said everything over and over. I probably do, too. Oh dear, I don't recognize anything." Helen lowered her window.

A dim light appeared and disappeared. I heard a foghorn. It is not necessarily a melancholy sound. I said, "Here, I'll lower my window. You're getting all wet."

ANTIQUES. FRESH VEGETABLES. TOURISTS.

"Right. No, I mean left. Right is the end of the beach."

A few lights pasted themselves against the windshield. The wipers smeared the lights. Our wheels sang through the water. I heard the ocean. We were the only car on the street.

Vacant lot. STONE HOTEL. HOTEL SPENCER. Vacant lot.

"Slow. Surely. Oh, lord."

"The Shore, Sea Crest," I read aloud. "Vacancy, Vacancy, No Vacancy." A blare of lights appeared. "Everybody must have gone somewhere, but somebody left the lights on. The Sea Gull. Baldwin's."

"We passed it. Back up. We passed it."

I reversed past Baldwin's, an elegant motel shaped like a T square, a bent arm embracing a swimming pool, past the Sea Gull, almost identical to Baldwin's, another T square, another pool.

"The cottage." She leaned over me. "There, the dark space between the two arms. Oh, my Lord. There's a driveway at the left. There should be. There used to be. Here. Turn. Turn right here, left."

I stopped Helen's car in the driveway. She was getting out. The light from the car showed broad steps that led to a screened porch. "Keys? You have your keys?"

"In my hand. I've been clutching them since before we got off the ferry." She stood in the rain. "Isn't that silly? I'm not really anxious. I'm just acting anxious."

She unlocked the screen door. "Don't bother with the luggage yet. We may not stay. But it's the place. It's the right place."

She had opened the front door and switched on a center light before I got to her. I had wanted to open the door for her. She turned quickly. "It's all right."

It was a beautiful place. I followed her from room to room, a long living room with windows on to the porch, a dining room: "Mama insisted on a dining room—we had a cook back then, a marvelous woman; her name was Lilac; but not this furniture; we had a round oak table; Mr. Kimberly has kept buying new pieces, and that's all right; Mama didn't mind at all; I don't mind"; a large kitchen, yellow and white: "The cupboard, that's Mama's old cupboard"; off the dining room, at the end of a little hall, a bathroom with gleaming fixtures: "Mama minded about the fixtures, they were expensive, but they're handsome, aren't they?"; off the hall two bedrooms: "This is the guest room, the furniture's the same; that's nice to think about; and the curtains look the same; they couldn't be, could they? I made them; I had a terrible cold and it was rainy; I hung them on July the Fourth, one of those years."

I said, "I thought this was supposed to be a cottage."

"It is." Helen was touching the curtains. She looked at me over her shoulder. "It's bigger than I remember. Isn't that wonderful, Ben? Nothing else ever has been, not before." She turned her head. "Everything else, everyplace else, has shrunk through the years."

I said, "Sure," and, "Yes." I expected her to cry.

Helen straightened her shoulders. She moved past me. I followed her into the living room.

"It's right. It's all just all right." She looked around the room. I wondered why I was feeling sorry for Helen Cunningham. I didn't have any reason. "Mr. Kimberly has done a splendid job, all these years. He was a young man then. Mama was right to trust him. And I still recognize a lot of things. That vase. It's funny, isn't it? The way things outlast us."

I said, "I have a chair from my father's office. Anita had it painted blue. It's in my office. I don't think I'm sentimental, but . . ."

"I'm not being sentimental. Don't let me be."

"Sentiment. That's different from sentimentality."

"This coffee table. That chair."

I said, "It's all great." I felt sorry for Helen.

I think it is wrong to go around feeling sorry for people. That's another thing I say, and Anita says, "You like to say that sort of thing, Ben."

I said, "That's an unusual banister, on the stairway there."

"I'd forgot. I'd completely forgot. Oh, Ben!" She was across the room, rubbing her hands on the banister. It was covered with shining rope. "I did it! And it was my idea! And it's lasted, all these years. Look at it. They must have varnished it every year. Just look."

She started up the steps, trailing her hand on the coiled rope. She was stately. Her hair had come loose. I thought, "She is beautiful and wanton." I was surprised at myself for thinking *wanton*. It was not a right word. I almost asked, "Am I supposed to follow you? Should I follow?"

Helen turned slowly in the center of the room. It was a big room, dormers at the back and on either side. A large window faced the ocean. There was a poster bed with a madras cover, a vanity dresser, two chests, a rocker, a little chair.

"The slipper chair. It was my great-great-grandmother's. And this was my room. Can you imagine it?" Helen was whispering. "Once I was fourteen years old, and I slept in that bed."

39

"It's a marvelous room."

Helen shook her head. She lifted her hands to her hair. She coiled her hair, rearranging two pins. She did not say, "I must look a mess." She said, "There were funny little bed lamps, with anchors on the shades. And a hooked rug. The floors were nice then. Oak. Mama was very proud of the floors. But you shouldn't expect everything to last. Anything. And it's all right. It's all all right."

"Maybe I ought to raise this window." I was an awkward man in a girl's bedroom.

"Please do. It's musty, isn't it? Houses get musty at the shore. They do everywhere, when they're closed up. But Mr. Kimberly has done a good job. Everything's nice, isn't it, Ben?"

The window opened easily. The ocean sounded loud, like hard breathing. I could not see the ocean. A car passed, sending up wings of water.

"I didn't tell you. Mama said the name of this cottage was Gulls and Buoys." Helen spelled the words. "She said she was going to have a sign put up out front. Mama teased me a lot. I was afraid she was serious. Mama was probably a wicked woman. Maybe we're all wicked. It's wicked to tease people."

I said, "It's hard to be fourteen."

"Of course. That's one of the hard ages. Among others. You can have this room, Ben. You can sleep up here if you want to."

She is a virgin, I thought. We are two old maids visiting together.

I thought about making love to Helen on the bed where she had once been fourteen. I said, "Of course not. The very idea. I'm a guest. Guests sleep in the guest room."

I was afraid.

Helen said, "You're welcome," and then she said, "We'd better bring in the stuff."

I told her I'd get it, there was no reason for us both either to drown or freeze to death. Helen said she would help. "I wish you'd brought a raincoat. At least put mine over your head."

I said, "A little rain never hurt anybody." I am often surprised at what a grown man can bring himself to say. "Anyhow, I'd look silly with a raincoat over my head."

Helen was laughing again. She held the screen door open while I brought the suitcases and groceries to the living room. Together we deposited the groceries in the kitchen, the empty luggage in Mama's room. I picked up Helen's suitcases. They were heavy. I complained. Helen said, "Get on with you. They're no heavier than when you put them in. I'm going to fix us hot drinks. You look blue at the gills." Her hair was loose again.

I had deliberately left my bag for last. In the kitchen Helen hummed a tune. I did not recognize the song. I wondered what words went with the melody. I put my suitcase on the bed in the guest bedroom. I took out my suit and hung it in the closet, put my shoes and slippers under the bed, my monogrammed pajamas and robe on top. I arranged my toilet things on the marble-topped dresser, the monogrammed razor box, the monogrammed toothbrush kit, memories of Christmases past for the man who has everything.

"It reminds you who you are," Anita says every Christmas. "If you catch amnesia you'll be able to identify yourself."

I did not say to myself that I was angry. Good old Ben Adams of the tidy compartments has a long history of not talking to himself until after an occasion, long after.

"Are you coming, Ben?"

I wished I were in bed with a woman. I wished the woman said, "Are you coming?" I said that much to myself. The woman in my mind was not Helen, not particularly. She was a woman I have never seen.

Helen still wore her raincoat. The teakettle on the stove sang. "Whatever have you been up to?"

"I've unpacked." I was cold. I was afraid I would start trembling, like a kid at a dirty movie.

"You didn't bring a sweater, I'll bet. Did you bring a sweater, Ben?"

"No ma'am. Thank you kindly, ma'am, but no ma'am."

I am tired of people who say at parties, "Every man wants to sleep with his mother." I am tired of all our easy talk. I wanted to sleep with a woman.

"Poor dear. I'm cold too. There should be electric heaters around here someplace. I wouldn't know where to look. We'll find them tomorrow. I don't know . . . yes, wait a minute." She handed me a

41

kitchen match. "Would you mind turning on the oven. Please?"

I turned on the old oven.

Helen's footsteps sounded on the stairs, and above me, and on the stairs, and behind me.

"Here."

She had brought me a blanket, pink with white silk binding. "For God's sake, Helen."

But I let her put the blanket around my shoulders.

"It's not your most becoming color, but it's attractive enough." Helen patted my shoulder.

I said, "I could be your mother, being taken care of."

"Don't say that."

"All right. I'm not saying it."

"Mr. Kimberly has thought of almost everything. The bed's made, mine is. I couldn't find the heaters. I hope yours is made."

"It is. I checked."

"Mr. Kimberly always insisted that Mama supply everything— linens, dishes, cooking stuff. He said he could rent to a better class of people that way. Why? I haven't the foggiest notion. I don't think other people supply everything. But now I'm glad. It's wonderful to step into a house with the beds made. The blankets are brand new. We used to have Hudson Bay blankets. Do you supply everything for your furnished apartments? Remind me to call Mr. Kimberly to-morrow, early. I've written him."

I thought of saying, "What is your favorite color? Who is your favorite movie star?"

I thought of saying, "We stall at making love, even at home, even married. Think of the hours people waste before making love."

I thought, "Who wins the Ridiculous Prize? Ben. Give me a *B,* give me a *E,* give me a *N.*" In Washington, Ben would be sitting in an expensive restaurant. "Input, output, thrust," the people around him would be saying.

Helen poured a little hot water into two pottery mugs. "It's mar-velous the way these mugs have lasted. We bought them in Berea, years ago." She filled the mugs with bourbon.

I said, "Isn't that a rather heavy portion?"

"Don't you want a rather heavy portion?"

"Please, ma'am. Yes, indeed, ma'am."

"Sugar? Lemon? We don't have cinnamon sticks. I used to make Mama a little toddy at night, at the last. It seemed to cheer her. She got so she looked forward to them."

"No, thanks. That will be fine. No sugar. No lemon."

Helen handed me a mug. Our hands did not touch.

"Anita thought of the lemon. I wouldn't have thought of it. We didn't get fresh things, just staples. The lemon comes in that plastic thing, shaped like a lemon. You're sure you don't want any? It's right here in the refrigerator. Anita is responsible for almost everything. I've never seen a mind like hers."

"Anita has a tidy mind."

"I think she won't be a bit surprised you came with me. I know she'll be pleased. Anita said—"

"Cheers."

"Cheers."

The drink was strong.

"Look." Helen waved her mug to the telephone that hung on the wall. "I hadn't noticed. I wrote him to have it installed. I hate to feel cut off. I'm sure it's working. Don't you want to call somebody?"

"Anita is in bed by now. She's long gone asleep. She doesn't expect me to call."

"I could call somebody. But I don't have anybody in the world to call. Except Mr. Kimberly. And I don't know his habits. He's probably long gone asleep, too. Isn't that strange to think about? A telephone and nobody to call?"

"We could check the time."

But we didn't.

We sat in a kitchen on two straight chairs, a man in a blanket and woman in a raincoat, their feet propped on an opened oven door. Helen talked. She could not seem to stop talking.

I yawned. I pretended to yawn.

Helen said, finally Helen said, "I know you're tired. It's been a long day's drive. You'll want to take a shower, a bath, try out the new fixtures. I have my little bath upstairs. I showed it to you, didn't I? I meant to show it to you. And you're sure you don't want another drink? Another drink might be good for you? It might help you sleep?"

I was tired. I assumed she meant exactly what she was saying. "Good enough. I'll take it with me."

43

"That's a good idea. I may do the same. You're sure you have everything?"

She fixed my drink. She handed it to me. I said, "Good night." She said, "Good night. I hope you sleep well." We did not even shake hands.

The fixtures worked well. I scrubbed my body hard. The soap, Mr Kimberly's soap I presumed, was a woman's soap. The bathroom smelled like funerals.

I dried myself hard. I stood naked in the bathroom. I drank to myself in the mirror. I drank to myself again and the drink was gone. It would have been pleasant to have thrown the mug hard against the floor.

It would break into a thousand pieces. Helen would come running downstairs. She would knock at the bathroom door. She would open the door. She would find me naked. The woman would look at the man's body. She would move toward the man.

I placed the mug carefully in the soap dish. I put on my pajamas and robe.

Before we were married I slept naked. Anita said, "That's fun. That's funny, Ben. But what if the house should burn down? You wouldn't want the house to burn down when you were nude, would you?" I started wearing pajamas. For a long time I teased Anita about the house's burning down. Sometimes I tell the story. Anita laughs as loudly as anyone.

The bed was comfortable. The sheets were clammy, but there were two pink blankets. I got out of bed and raised a window. I could hear the ocean. I had forgotten the ocean.

When I was young I said my prayers every night. I kneeled by the bed; I folded my hands; I closed my eyes tight enough to see rainbows. My father saw to it that I said my prayers. "Have you said your prayers, Ben?" Prayer was always plural.

Sometimes I was already asleep when he came into my room. I found it difficult, almost impossible, to lie to my father. "No, not really. Just to myself."

44

"Well, get out of that bed. Say your damn prayers, the way they teach you at church."

For years I said my prayers.

In Helen's mama's guest room I said, "Goddamn, goddamn, goddamn."

I went to sleep. I dreamed hard dreams. I dreamed I was in bed with somebody who was saying my name.

I don't know what time I woke. It was very dark. For a minute I couldn't remember where I was.

I had to go to the bathroom. I started not to flush the toilet. I thought, "I don't want to disturb Helen." I thought, "You dumb son of a bitch." I flushed the toilet. I flushed it again. It was difficult to hear the toilet over the ocean. I brushed my teeth.

I'm sure Helen did not call me, I'm almost sure.

I woke because I had to go to the bathroom. And then I went down the little hall to the dining room, to the living room, to the porch, because I wanted to look out. I'm almost sure Helen did not call, but I was not surprised to see her at the end of the porch.

She sat in a tall-backed rocker. She held a mug in her hand. She was wrapped in a blanket.

"Ben?"

"I didn't mean to scare you. Were you expecting somebody else?"

"You didn't scare me. I'm having another toddy. I couldn't sleep. Don't you want one?"

I sat in a rocker next to Helen. The porch was cluttered with rockers. They looked like people, swaying. "I can get my own. In a minute."

"You shouldn't be out here without your slippers. You should have brought a blanket. You'll catch your death."

I said, "Somebody was always telling me I was going to catch my death. Of something." I was trembling.

"Here. Take a drink of this."

"Thank you." I held the mug with both hands. I finished the drink.

I am sure I reached for Helen first. I am not trying to remember myself as particularly in charge of the situation, or manly, or aggressive.

I have read too many novels. Humanist businessmen read too much. All of the men on the Washington committee speak knowingly of the books they have read. They speak of sex casually. We pretend that every man, ourselves, is an expert cocksman. On occasion, everybody is named Ernie.

I placed my hand on the back of her chair. The chair rocked forward. We were standing. She called my name against my mouth.

I want to suspect Anita.

Helen was naked under the blanket. I said, "My God, you're naked." I was shocked. I was embarrassed at being shocked. I said, "Come on. Goddamn it, come on."

Perhaps I was a figure in a television comedy.

"Ben, Ben, Ben." We were walking awkwardly together, still kissing. I almost tripped at the doorsill. I thought I was leading Helen. But we were moving toward the stairway. The blanket fell. I pulled my mouth away.

"Here."

Helen turned away from me. I held the blanket for her. She pressed herself back against me. "Thank you," she said, as if I were helping her with a cape after a dinner party.

I thought about laughing. I said, "Goddamn you, Helen."

I pushed her into the dining room, the hall, to the guest room. I pushed hard. She kept saying, "Ben, Ben, Ben."

I said, "We're sleeping in here tonight."

I suppose I had not imagined a woman like Helen.

I have thought on such occasions, on a few occasions, "We are doing this. Now we'll do this." I suppose I have always *thought*.

She kept saying, "Quick, quick, Ben."

I stopped thinking.

I am not sure why I am writing this.

I am a recorder.

I can remember words. I am a tape, recording. I could record moans and cries.

46

She was a long time coming. But I was stronger than I have ever been. When she came, her voice was a whinny. She was biting my lips. She held me so tightly I could not move. I was shouting. I was trying to pull away from her. I managed to get hold of her arms. I wrenched at her. I was afraid I was hurting her. I hoped I was hurting her.

I am embarrassed by the books Ernie gives me to read. I would like to imagine myself a hero. "Great. Good," I say to Ernie, placing the book on his desk.

"What about that!" Ernie says, not a question, an exclamation. Ernie keeps his books in a locked file drawer. "There are plenty more where that came from."

"Thanks. Thanks, Ernie. I'll be calling on you."

Ernie's eyes are slimy. When he looks at a woman his eyes slide over her. I have resented the way he has looked at Anita. I do not imagine Anita and Ernie in bed together. I am trying to imagine them together.

I said, "Are you all right?"

"I'm lovely. Thank you. Thank you so much."

I lay beside her. She was kissing me. "Lovely, lovely, lovely."

"Here. Put your head on my shoulder."

"Wait. Wait just a minute."

I said, "Come on." I was exhausted. I do not like to admit exhaustion. I pulled the covers over us. I settled two pillows under my head.

Her head was heavy on my shoulder. She said something against my chest. I imagined being as deaf as my father just before he died. I do not think I am going deaf. I had rather be deaf than blind. I can imagine living in a world where mouths move without sound.

"Was it lovely for you, too?"

I said, "Lovely." I kissed her forehead.

"You're perspiring. You're wet all over. Let me get a towel."

"Lie still."

She said, "Were you thinking about anything else? While we were making love?"

I said, "Having sex." I did not say *fucking*.

"Yes, 'having sex.' I'm sorry. I can't say words very easily."

47

I said, "I suppose I can't either. It's ridiculous. A word is just a word."

"We're nice people, aren't we, Ben?"

"Very nice. Nice." I was shocking myself.

"It was very important to Mama for people to be nice. It's still an important word."

"I'm not so very nice. I've trained myself to pretend." I made myself say the word again. "Nice."

"But sometimes I wish I were the kind of woman who called a spade a 'damned dirty shovel.' That was one of Mama's jokes. It was her one suggestive joke."

After a while she said, "But were you?"

"Was I what?"

"Thinking about somebody else, about another time, 'having sex'?"

"No. I'm not now." I was telling the truth. I listened only to the words we said and our breathing.

"I'm glad."

"You were thinking about something else, somebody else." I was jealous. I wanted to laugh at myself. I said, "I'm jealous," listening to our recording in the dark room. I laughed.

"I don't have anything to think about."

I was laughing. I said, "Everybody who believes that stand on his head. I mean, 'their heads.' That's what we used to say in grade school."

"I mean it."

"You don't just wake up knowing how to make love, excuse the expression. Not the way you make it. You're a very funny girl, a very phony virgin, excuse the expression." I was pinching her breast. Perhaps I wanted to hurt her. I wanted the recording to cry out.

"I mean it. It's true. It's always true." She was moving her hands over me again. "For an old maid it's always the first time."

The woman said, "Your . . . you have a very lovely . . . it's very lovely. Are you feeling guilty?"

The man said, "No, of course not."

"I'm not either. I won't if you won't. Promise."

48

"Cross my heart and hope to die," I said. "And I imagine I am lying in my teeth. Who promises about guilt? I may be a little slow at it."

The woman said, "Lovely, lovely." We were kissing again.

I did not think about Anita. I did not *not* think about Anita.

The man said, "I'm not having fantasies. I'm not fantasizing, if that's what you mean. There isn't time with you. This is the fantasy."

"Glad, glad," Helen said.

When I woke I knew where I was. Before I allowed myself to open my eyes I thought, "I am at Helen Cunningham's cottage in Cape May. Last night I had sex with Helen Cunningham. It was good. Even if your bones ache and you are a little hungover, you are very splendid."

I reached for Helen. Always in the morning I reach for Anita before I open my eyes.

I was alone in the bed in the guest room.

A vague brick wall, a motel, faced the window in front of me. The Sea Gull. The window at the rear of the house held a yard full of fog.

I was proud of myself for not calling to Helen. A man can tell, he should be able to tell, when he is alone in a house.

I thought, "We missed the boat, and I am facing a brick wall, and I am in a fog." I was smiling. I delight in the comfort of clichés. Once named, they are almost never true.

I had made the boat rather gloriously. The windows opened to daylight.

But before I dressed and shaved I checked the house. Helen was not upstairs in her room. The drapes were drawn at all the windows. Her bed was unmade. The room could have been an underwater photograph. The posts of the bed rose delicately. In the kitchen, coffee simmered on a hot plate. The oven was turned on, the door opened.

Helen had left a note on the kitchen table: "Good morning. I'm off to town. Do make yourself at home."

Anita always signs her notes with two rows of *X*'s under a smile face. The girls are fond of smile faces, too. They applied smile

49

stickers to both the Buick and the Volkswagen. They were furious with their father when he had the decals removed at the service station.

I had never seen Helen's handwriting before. Her note filled a full page of writing paper. It was half longhand, half printed. I smiled a smile face at the handwriting.

I was dressed when the bell sounded. I had not noticed a doorbell when we arrived. I was ashamed of myself. I thought I had been noticing everything.

I assumed the sound was Helen.

I put my coffee cup on the refrigerator and rushed to the porch. Mr. Kimberly wore a Hawaiian shirt that trailed yellow hibiscus. I felt foolish in my dark suit. At least I wore no necktie. I felt foolish for my eagerness and my vanity.

"I'm Frank Kimberly." He stood on the top step, holding the screen door open. "Is Helen here? Miss Cunningham?" The screen door banged behind him. "We've got to put a silencer on that door." He was shaking my hand. His hand was soft. He was a short, fat man, younger than I had expected. He could have been the son of the man at the ferry booth.

It does not take many people to make a life.

I introduced myself. I said, "Helen is a longtime friend of my wife. I came down with her last night. Drove down." I disliked Mr. Kimberly. He waited until I said, "My wife insisted. You know how wives are."

I am too old for such awkwardness.

I followed him into the living room.

"You folks find everything all right, right?"

"Yes. Miss Cunningham was pleased."

"I had one of the nigra ladies, Pearl, in all day yesterday. She's pretty good at cleaning." Mr. Kimberly ran his hands over the mantel. He studied his fingertips. "She's pretty good. I've had her four-five years now." I assumed he spoke sexually. Perhaps he did. "Yes sir, it looks pretty good. This is a nice house. Helen won't have any trouble selling, Miss Cunningham, for a good price, a real good price." He was in the dining room. "Whatever you need, you give me a buzz. You tell Helen. Cigar?"

"No, thank you. I've given up. It's a year now." I disliked myself for sounding prissy.

"One man's poison," Mr. Kimberly said. "Everybody's scared of something."

I watched him unwrap his cigar. He bit the end, blowing the tip into his hand. "Ashtray? Here we are. I told the nigra to see you had everything." He rolled his cigar in his mouth. His Weimaraner eyes moved slowly around the room.

Ernie tends to all of our rentals now. I thought of Ernie. "Heaters," I said. "Miss Cunningham was looking for heaters."

Mr. Kimberly snapped his fingers. I couldn't remember when I had seen a man snap his fingers.

"I knew I'd forget something. They're up at the house. I bet you folks were cold last night. This is some weather."

"No, not particularly." Mr. Kimberly and I looked at each other. We held each other's eyes. I would have liked to say, "We slept together." I said, "She'll be back in a little while. She ran uptown—downtown. I don't have my directions yet. Won't you sit down?"

"I don't care if I do. We can visit a little. Helen's a mighty fine lady, and her mother before her. I was just a little tyke when the Cunninghams built. My daddy sold them the lot. He was their contractor, too." Mr. Kimberly had led me back to the porch. He sat down heavily. "I used to tag along with him. I guess I know Cape May better than any man alive. You got boys?"

"No, girls. We have twin girls."

"Six boys." Mr. Kimberly nodded. He struck a match, but he did not light his cigar. "They're limbs of Satan. But I think the world and all of them. The missus says if they change the rules she'll give three of them back to the pope. She's the limit."

If Helen had not arrived, I would have . . . I would have gone on listening to Mr. Kimberly.

He finally lighted his cigar.

Helen arrived with packages, a grocery sack, two sacks from Tevis's Men's Shoppe, a box from Cape Bake. I took the packages from her.

51

"Mr. Kimberly, how nice. I just stopped in at your office. How very nice."

Nice is a dirty word. It soils a person's mouth.

They were shaking hands. I had expected them to kiss.

Mr. Kimberly said, "How long has it been? You haven't changed a bit. Yes, maybe you have. Maybe you're prettier. What do you say, Ben? Don't you think maybe she's prettier?"

I said, "Without a doubt."

Helen smiled at me. I imagined her smile as no more intimate than a bumper sticker. I was annoyed with her. I wanted Mr. Kimberly to assume we were lovers.

"Ben and I were just chewing the rag. He said you thought the place looked all right. Those heaters. I'll get 'em to you right away."

"Marvelous. You've been marvelous. Sit down. Please sit down. Both of you."

Helen manages, even though she does not give the impression of managing. At home I would have carried the packages back to the kitchen, leaving Anita to handle the bore. But I didn't want to leave them alone together. I held the packages in my arms.

I am a comic character.

"And the town, the mall, absolutely marvelous. I adore what's happened to the town. At first I was almost frightened—I didn't recognize anything. And then I drove around a little—the houses, the marvelous Victorian houses."

"Our future is in our past," Mr. Kimberly said.

"The gingerbread. I've always adored the gingerbread—I mean carpenter's lace. It always made Mama furious for me to call it gingerbread."

"Your mother was a fine lady. I was just saying so." Mr. Kimberly did not cross himself, but he gave the impression of a man about to cross himself.

Helen asked about the Kimberly boys. She said she treasured their photographs on the Christmas cards, Mama had saved every card. She asked about old Mrs. Kimberly: surely the summer weather would be good for her arthritis. And young Mrs. Kimberly? She seemed genuinely interested in the life of the foolish little pot-bellied man.

At least Mr. Kimberly had the grace to refuse coffee and sweet

52

roll. He had a million things to tend to, he was busier than a bird dog, he was glad to have made my acquaintance, he would be seeing us, it was fine to have Helen back in town. He did not ask how long I was going to stay. I put the packages on the floor, and we all shook hands again. "You call me if you need anything. You be sure and call me."

I picked up my packages, feeling foolish.

I wanted to quarrel with Helen. She waved to Mr. Kimberly from the front steps. Helen is so much taller than Anita, she looked vast. She raised her arm high and waved. Her profile against the fog was magnificent. I thought, "She's a lot of woman." Those are Ernie's words.

"Hurry," Helen said. She took the Tevis's packages from me. "Put those others anywhere—the dining room table." She was halfway up the stairway. She stopped and smiled at me, her hand touching the rope banister. She said, "Surprise."

I said, "You are magnificent."

She stood by the poster bed. She was pulling something orange from one of the packages. "No, don't look, Ben. Close your eyes."

"What is this? What's going on?"

We were kissing. For a long time we were kissing. She pushed me away. "Close your eyes."

I closed my eyes. I was in grade school. Mrs. Phalp, the best housekeeper, companion, attendant, cook, whatever the word, mistress, my father ever employed, said, "Open your eyes, Ben." It was my birthday. I was thirteen. It was Saturday. I had slept late. My father stood behind Mrs. Phalp.

He was smiling when I opened my eyes.

Mrs. Phalp was with us less than two years. She died of cancer. For two months I visited her in the hospital. "Don't cry, Ben," my father said. "Men don't cry. Damn it, stop crying. There'll be somebody else."

She had bought me a catcher's mitt and a blue sleeveless sweater.

On Helen's bed, spread out as if in a store window, lay an orange cardigan and a brown sports shirt.

"Try them on. Hurry, Ben."

"My gosh."

"Hurry. I never had so much fun. The man said, 'Father's Day?' I said, 'Of course.' 'Yes, of course,' I said. The man said, 'Have a nice day.' He was a young man. He looked like you, a little."

I said, "They fit perfectly." I said, "You shouldn't have. A fool and her money." I said what birthday people are supposed to say.

"They look marvelous, Ben. They're your colors." She ran her hands over my shoulders.

I said, "They're elegant. Thank you. Thank you so much." I was glad they were not monogrammed.

"Take them off, Ben. Hurry."

The zipper on her dress was an anchor. She was naked under her dress. She threw her dress on the bed. She threw my orange sweater and my brown shirt and my trousers and underwear on the bed. We made love on our clothes.

Having sex in the underwater light of the morning was different from the dark love of the night before. Always Anita and I have made love in darkness. At night a man's wife could be any woman.

Helen Cunningham's hair against the orange sweater was beautiful. Her breasts were smaller and less firm than Anita's, her hips larger. "More welcoming," I thought. And I stopped thinking.

Perhaps I slept again. Perhaps we both slept.

Helen said, "It must be twelve o'clock. It must be noon." She spoke as if she did not lie in my arms. We could have been people on a patio, among other people, planning an outing. "Hurry, Ben. We have to go to the beach. Imagine! We've been here this long and we haven't been to the beach."

I checked my wristwatch on the bedside table. The hands said twelve. I said, "You know what time it is."

I watched Helen. She walked to one of the chests. She opened the second drawer. She took a black bathing suit and a white beach coat from the drawer. She turned.

I said, "I'm a voyeur. I'm a voyeur watching you."

She said, "I'm glad."

I said, "You're brown. I'm ashamed of being so white."

She said, "I've been working at it." She said, "I'm too shy for a bikini. I'm working at that, too. I want to get over being shy."

I said, "You're very shy."

She stepped into her suit slowly, smiling at me. I am used to modesty, a washcloth over the breasts. I said, "Slowly. Very slowly."

Very slowly she pulled her suit to her waist. She cupped her breasts in her hands. She said, "Look at me." She rubbed her palms over her breasts.

"I'm looking." I was excited.

"I like for you to look at me." Slowly she raised her suit. "I'm looking at you. You're lovely." Slowly she put on her beach coat.

I reached for my shorts. I said, "Perhaps I should cover my loveliness."

"No need, no need at all. On the beach they'll flock to you. But hurry, Ben." She was pulling my clothes from under me.

I like to remember our laughing together.

Carrying my clothes, Helen led me downstairs. She stood in the doorway of the guest room while I put on my trunks. "Slowly, very slowly," Helen said, laughing. "And here's your becoming new sport shirt. You must wear your shirt until we get across the road, clear to the beach. They're strict about modesty here at Cape May. At least they used to be. We mustn't be immodest."

Everything was very funny.

"Bon voyage," Helen said in the living room. She leaned against me.

"Bon voyage. Have a nice time at the beach."

We walked slowly down the flagstones to the street. "We missed the azaleas. But the hydrangeas, look, Ben. Admire everything, Ben. Don't miss anything."

The hydrangeas around the porch were pink and blue and purple. "I'm admiring. The grass is very green."

"It's nice to know the grass is green on our side. It's not always greener on the other side. Not always. The motels, look: their grass is gray."

We crossed the street to the steps beside the macadam walk.

Helen took my arm. "It isn't a boardwalk any more. I noticed that much driving to town. But I didn't look at the ocean this morning." Helen closed her eyes. She held tightly to my arm. "I've been saving the ocean. I've always made something of first looks. And last looks. First look, Ben."

"My," I said. Helen said, "Oh, my."

The beach was broad. The waves came in. The water moved back to the sky. The sun covered us.

Helen said, "I wouldn't recognize it. But that's all right. There have been hurricanes. Hurry, Ben."

She was running across the beach, taking off her coat as she ran. She dropped her coat and kicked away her sandals. I folded my new shirt and placed it on top of her coat.

The water was cold. I didn't want to go into the water. I had thought we would lie on the beach for a while. I thought of turning back to the beach.

"Hurry, Ben." Already she was in to her waist. She dived into a breaking wave. In a moment she was farther out than any of the bathers.

A kid with an air mattress bumped into me. I was angry with the boy. I splashed water on my shoulders. A wave caught me. I swore at the wave. The boy said, "What the hell, mister!"

From the beach came a shrill whistle. The lifeguard was standing in his chair. He was motioning for Helen to come back in. I called, "Helen, Helen!" but of course she didn't hear me. I was embarrassed that she was being reprimanded.

The guard was at the edge of the water. He blew his whistle angrily.

I imagined Helen dead.

The lifeguard was beside me, to his knees in the water, when Helen turned. She swam toward us, waving.

I shouted, "Get in here."

The guard blew his whistle again.

I said, "She's coming. Can't you see she's coming?"

The guard said, "This isn't any day for swimming. There's a bad backwash." He was half a head taller than I am. He wore red trunks and a white T-shirt; he was a handsome boy, very dark.

I said, "She was swimming here before you were born. She knows this place."

"Sorry, sir," he said. "You tell her. This isn't any day for swimming."

"Isn't it absolutely perfect?" Helen lifted her hands to push back her hair.

I said, "You might have drowned. The lifeguard said—"

"Silly. Lifeguards are old maids."

But we stayed with the other bathers. We fought the waves. I said, "You're the only woman I ever saw who was beautiful with wet hair."

"Tell me. Tell me again." She was laughing again.

I waited until Helen suggested that we get out of the water. "About ready?"

A wave knocked me flat. I had been ready to go in for a long time.

Helen lay on her coat, I on my new shirt. I felt quiet and, I suppose, safe. I felt very safe. The sun was a benediction.

Helen said, "We forgot our sunglasses. We forgot towels. We forgot to eat. You must be starved."

I said, "I'm asleep. We haven't forgot anything."

"Oh, Ben."

Anita has always said that the first day on a beach is the longest day in time. Anita is right. I kept being grateful that the day stretched long. I slept among comfortable voices.

A beach changes. It's not only the tide of water, it's the people.

When I woke, the beach was no longer middle-aged couples and baby-sitting grandmothers; it was young couples and their own young children.

A boy, twelve maybe, an impressionable age, with an oyster shell drew a vast vague circle in the sand. He walked the circle three times while his parents watched. The parents were small, almost as

57

small as the boy; they looked exactly like each other. The boy skipped around the circle while they watched, nudging each other. "Oh, what fun," the man or the woman said. The boy raced the circle until he fell. He did not manage to run twice the circle. The woman, or the man, fell into the other's arms.

"What do you think of that?" the boy said.

His parents were too convulsed to answer him.

Two black children filled a toy dumptruck with sand. Making truck noises they scooted the truck to the edge of the sea.

A little girl with bright hair asked her mother, whose hair was whiter than the sun, "Let me get some water." She carried a yellow bucket, painted with daisies, to the water. She carried the bucket to her mother. She tripped. There wasn't any water left in the bucket. "For Christ sake," the mother said, pulling her bra even farther down on her breasts.

"Let's get out of here."

Helen said, "You've had a lovely nap."

I did not like to think about being watched while I slept.

I resent open caskets at funerals.

I am thinking more about Aunt Della than I mean to think.

"You're hungry, Ben. Did you bring money? I didn't. We'll have a good lunch."

We went back to the cottage for money.

On the porch, going in and out, we kissed. We scratched at each other. "Hurry, Ben."

Across the street, by our steps to the boardwalk, sat a vast man, or boy.

I said, "What a strangely shaped head." I wasn't thinking.

"He's afflicted."

There were three of them, four, seven. I couldn't count them. A row of knapsacks edged the boardwalk. Two of the men, the boys, tried to open knapsacks. They wore khaki shorts and shirts. The boys' mouths hung loose. Their heads were almost shaved. A young man, as handsome as one of the lifeguards, said, "Go on, Charlie, you can do it."

I said, "My God, it's a mongoloid convention."

"It's a school or something."

I touched Helen's arm. "We'll cross up there. At the next steps."

But Helen was walking up our steps.

I do not think Helen waved and spoke first.

Three of the boys waved at her, the way children wave, lifting their shoulders, snapping their fingers against their palms.

Helen waved back, the way a child waves. "Hello, hello. Good afternoon."

I nodded to the crippled figures.

When we were on the sand Helen said, "Something. Something always comes up to say . . ."

"To say what?"

"Poor dears."

I am writing a meditation on being blessed.

I am writing a goddamned meditation.

Helen pointed out the Windsor and the Congress, fine sprawling old hotels.

We ate on the deck of a restaurant near Convention Hall.

We walked. We walked back, clear to the concrete ship beyond the lighthouse.

Helen spoke to people on the beach. "Good afternoon. Lovely day," she said. It was not a lovely day. The fog appeared and disappeared. Fat pale beachgoers sat like plaster figures under umbrellas they did not need. "Hello, you darlings," Helen said to the children whose parents and grandparents smiled back at her.

I looked for the afflicted boys, but they had disappeared.

"It's the way I remember, almost the way," Helen said. "It's a family beach still. I hate beaches where everybody is one age, young. Cape May has a lot of grandmothers. They make me feel svelte."

I said, "You know—"

"No, Ben, no compliments. Not when I've asked for them. I've taken pretty good care of my body. I haven't had much else to take care of. Not regularly."

I imagined lovers. I was jealous of the lovers. I suppose a man,

59

pretending acceptance of the world, should be surprised at jealousy. I was surprised.

I am a dishonest man, pretending dishonesty.

We stood by the concrete ship. Three little girls chased one another in the waves. "They're nice people, aren't they? The people here?"

I said, "Very nice. Nice, nice, *nice.*" I liked to say the word.

A girl and a boy lay together on a blanket. The girl lay on the boy's arm. She wore a bikini that was too small for her. The boy had an erection. Helen turned her head as we walked by.

Helen said, "They weren't very nice."

"What do you mean? I don't understand what you mean."

"You know what I mean."

"I'm surprised you didn't stop and engage them in conversation."

"That's not fair, Ben. I haven't spoken to anybody, not really. Except The Twins."

I thought, "I am relaxed. I am laughing in the fog." The fog was like going blind.

Helen stopped to speak to the old lady we had already nodded to on our way up the beach. The old lady was painting in oil a picture of the sky and the sea. She sat in a canvas chair. She wore a broad-brimmed straw hat and a flowered dress. The picture was a child's drawing of the scene: scalloped waves and cotton-puff clouds. But the scene itself was like a child's drawing.

"My, you're coming along well," Helen said. She did not let go of my hand.

"Thank you. Thank you very much." The old lady held her canvas board away from her. "Yes, it is coming along. Do you paint?" She wore a name tag on her flat breast.

"No, but I'd love to. It's a marvelous picture, isn't it, Ben?"

"Marvelous."

"I paint everywhere I go." She patted her name tag. "I'm Mrs. Herbert Lanning. Toronto. Baptist. I'm here for the Global Congress." The printing on her label agreed with her.

"We're the Adamses," Helen said easily. "Helen and Ben."

60

"I saw you go past. I admired you when you went past. You both hold yourselves so well." She was painting again, adding another scallop to the sea. "Have you been to the meetings?"

"We just got here."

"You should come to the tabernacle. We're having wonderful speakers. You'll be very welcome. Tonight there's a very famous preacher, from South America somewhere, but he speaks beautiful English. He's preaching tomorrow morning, too. We have two services a day, with conferences thrown in. I'm playing hooky this afternoon."

"How very nice. We couldn't go tonight. We're busy. But you're good to ask us."

I pulled at Helen's hand. I wanted to laugh. Or I felt I should be wanting to laugh.

"It's a two-week congress. I'll look for you. We sit in sections marked with our countries. There are an awful lot of people from Africa. They're as nice as they can be. But you come to the Canada section. The tabernacle holds two thousand people."

"Thank you. Thank you very much. It's nice to meet you."

I said, "Nice, nice."

"It's nice to meet you both, Mr. and Mrs. Adams." She did not turn her head. "Have a good walk."

"Good-bye, good-bye," Helen said.

I said, "Really."

Helen dropped my hand. "No, don't." She was shaking her head, her beautiful head.

Helen's eyes are very dark. We were looking at each other. For a moment I thought Helen looked old, almost as old as the painting lady. The lines around her mouth and eyes were deep.

"What goes?"

"Nothing. I was just hoping you wouldn't think the old lady was . . . funny."

"Who's laughing?"

"Nobody. You're a darling, Ben." She took my hand again.

"Mr. and Mrs. Adams. How about that?"

"Wasn't it fun? You didn't mind, did you?"

"I'm delighted. I'm flattered. I hadn't known."

"She wouldn't have thought we were nice if I'd said otherwise."

61

"We're nice, all right. We've already decided we're nice."

"I could get pretty good at lying. I looked her straight in the eyes. We made her feel good. She's probably thinking about us right now. She's glad we're having such a nice time."

I thought about the word *guilt*.

We swam again, at our beach. Already it was our beach. Already I was recognizing people, the cross-eyed little girl with the thick glasses, the grandmother with the purple suit and the varicose veins, the man with the American flag tattooed on his arm.

We dried in the sun again.

In the cottage, in my bathroom, we showered together. Anita and I have never bathed together. I am sorry.

I shaved again.

Helen was dressed first. She stood in the doorway of my room. She wore a linen dress the color of her hair, a yellow belt. Her purse and shoes were yellow.

I said, "Very nice. You look like an advertisement for something, for an elegant woman. What do I wear to live up to you?"

"Underwear, but slowly. A shirt, trousers. Slowly, very slowly."

She did not lean against the doorway. She stood straight. Anita leans in doorways. "Isn't it nice we have secrets together? Already we have secrets and family sayings."

I said, "I was thinking about secrets. They're necessary. After a while you don't have secrets."

Anita would have said, "The very idea. What a thing to say!"

Helen said, "That's probably true. It's an unfortunate truth. You probably know better than I do. But I know it."

It has been a long time since Anita and I have had any new secrets together.

Perhaps that is the trouble with marriages that have lasted for eighteen years of getting along and getting along and getting along.

The secrets become family sayings.

62   I said, "You tell them. They wear out. If you don't have new secrets . . ."

"Perhaps it's not impossible."

I brushed my hair with my monogrammed brushes. "Should I wear a tie to dinner? I want to be nice."

"No tie. And we're eating here. I'll pick up a steak at the grocery. And you have to see the town. Imagine being here all day and not seeing the marvelous houses."

"We're going to a bar, and dinner, and maybe a nightclub. People always dress up and go out when they're on vacation."

"Please, Ben. It isn't a very long vacation."

I held the brushes in my hands and looked at Helen. I lifted my arms. I said, "You are a woman of your own mind. I seem to be attracted to women of their own minds." I heard myself asking, "You wouldn't tell anybody, would you?" I was surprised at myself.

Helen did not say, "Tell what, Ben? Tell what, for goodness' sake?"

She said, "No. I couldn't. Even if there were somebody to tell. Whom would I tell?"

I was embarrassed. I said, "You're the only person I know who says *whom* so well. You say *however,* too. I don't know many people who say *however.*"

"Who would I tell?"

"Nobody. I wasn't thinking. I'm going to wear a tie and a jacket."

I thought of saying, "I love you." Anita, the girls, even I say, "I love you." "I love you, too," we say it as naturally as we answer "Good morning" or "Good night."

When we embraced and kissed, Helen did not say, "Careful, you're messing me; watch out for my hair, Ben; don't get lipstick on yourself." She wiped the lipstick from my mouth and kissed me again.

We were the most dressed-up people in the supermarket. "You certainly look like a dude," Helen said. I said, "Thank you very much, Miss Universe." We thought we were funny.

It was a pleasant store. The Muzak played Cole Porter tunes. I pushed the cart. I couldn't remember when I had last been in a supermarket. Anita markets on Friday morning.

"Thank you very much," I said every time Helen deposited something in my basket.

A large woman in white socks and bedroom slippers said, "You aren't going to buy that lettuce, are you? You aren't going to let them rob you for that lettuce? And asparagus? Not asparagus!"

"Doctor's orders. My wife requires them."

"I guess it takes us all."

It was a happy time. I was happy.

At the checkout counter I reached for my billfold. The pictures of the girls looked at me. They are old pictures. Helen was already paying. I started to protest. The woman in the white socks was behind me. I thought she could have been somebody Helen knew a long time ago, a cleaning lady perhaps. For a moment I imagined every person in the line was somebody Helen had known. "Miss Helen," "Why, Helen Cunningham, where in the world did you come from?" "Helen, darling," they would say. I imagined Mr. Kimberly at the next counter. But the man was thinner; he did not resemble Mr. Kimberly at all.

I put my billfold in my pocket. I said, "Thank you very much, Mrs. Adams."

"My pleasure," Helen said.

I paid for the gin and tonics we had on the Victorian Village mall. We sat in uncomfortable white iron chairs at a white table under a yellow umbrella. "Yes, charming, yes," I said. "Yes, somebody certainly had vision. Yes, indeed." Helen was delighted with the mall.

I said, "It's strange you don't see somebody you know. I would expect . . ."

"It would be nice, wouldn't it? But my mother's friends are dead now, all of them." For a moment her eyes were blank.

"I wasn't meaning anything."

"And it wouldn't matter anyhow. If everybody I've ever known in my life came in and sat near us—that couldn't matter. We have a secret, you remember. Whatever anyone would guess, or imply, or wonder—we still have our secret."

She put her hand over mine. She wore a ring with a yellow stone. We were a Victorian novel. I wasn't following her logic. I was anxious, and annoyed with myself.

I do not like for people to know what I am thinking.

Helen said, "You're looking good. You got some sun today. You look good, Ben."

"And you're turned to gold."

"We are full of compliments. This is a complimentary day."

The houses were as marvelous as Helen had promised. She drove slowly through the tree-lined streets, pausing here and there. Many of the places were ridiculous: turrets, cupolas, layers and circles of porches, and always the white lacework; the houses stood glowing white, pink, yellow, blue, side by side with houses that could have happened anywhere.

"There. Look." Helen stopped the car. "Ours could be like that. Add a porch upstairs. And gingerbread. I would have it dripping with gingerbread." Helen allowed the car to move back into the street. "I said *ours,* didn't I? I didn't mean to. *My. Mine.* I wasn't meaning to be romantic, or forward, or flirting, or . . . I wasn't thinking."

"They're so much like Valentines, that's why." I was not troubled. "Or wedding cakes."

"That's right. Exactly. That's what they're like."

Helen talked well about the houses. I felt as if I had never looked at a Victorian home before: the picket fences, the carved posts, the dormers, the arched and pointed windows, the fish-scale ornamental shingles, the captains' walks and the widows' walks. "Mansard, American Gothic, castellated, Italian Renaissance—there, the pink one—all the styles together."

I said, "Maybe that's what Victorian means."

Helen said, "I guess maybe I'm Victorian. Or want to be."

I did not smile. She was being serious. "Well, I wouldn't say exactly."

"Not that. You're Victorian, Ben. I think you are. It's not a bad word. It's just a way of getting along."

I said, "I'm attracted to those houses."

I thought of the slabs of wood and glass that Anita and I live among. "When you tell me about them, I'm attracted."

"Those bargeboards, the trim under the eaves. That's only ornamental. It doesn't pretend to be anything else."

65

I said, "You could really hide away in that house. And that one."
I didn't exactly know what we were talking about, but it was pleasant to drive down the cool green street. I said, "I can imagine a fine Victorian gentleman holing up behind that dormer and writing himself a great piece of pornography."

Helen did not answer for half a block. "Okay. All right. That too."

We had turned into the far end of Beach Drive. Helen pointed out the tabernacle where our Baptist lady attended the Global Congress. At least two dozen flags, from all the world, fluttered over the lawn.

We stopped in front of the red-and-white Sea Mist, where four or five porches rose to a cupola with an American flag.

I said, "It's great. It's all great."

"What time is it? No, don't tell me."

"I couldn't tell you. I left my wristwatch in the bathroom. That was a great bath."

Helen was laughing. We were laughing together again.

I am sorry I forget the laughter that happens with making love.

I would like to change the world. I would like to change my whole goddamned life.

I said, "We'll walk on the beach again before we eat."

"I made you say that."

"Of course you did. I am pretending to assert myself."

"Ben, Ben, Ben."

I liked to hear Helen's calling my name.

"Helen, Helen."

We stopped by the cottage only to get my new sweater and leave our shoes. It was a pleasure to watch Helen take down her panty hose. "Slowly, Helen. Very slowly."

The beach was almost deserted, a boy and two dogs, an old man and an old lady. I keep remembering an old man and an old lady, always walking: I cannot remember their faces.

Helen spoke to them. "Good evening. Lovely evening."

The tide was coming in, but the beaches were still wide.

Barefoot, we walked the side of every jetty, into the waters of

66

every beach. The water was cold. My sweater felt good. "Don't you want to wear my sweater?"

"Of course not. It's your sweater."

We walked up to the boardwalk at Convention Hall. "Not sidewalk, Ben—*boardwalk*. In honor of the olden days."

The benches were crowded with old men and women, many of them wearing hats, old women alone, young families, teen-age clusters, children everywhere, all watching one another.

"It's not Atlantic City," Helen said. "It's more like a PTA carnival."

I nodded, wondering what she knew of PTA carnivals.

"I know about PTA carnivals," she said as if I had spoken. "All my friends in Indianapolis have children. *Had* children, carnival-aged. I'm a professional aunt as well as a professional daughter. I'm the queen of carnivals." Her voice broke. Or I imagined her voice broke. She was smiling, however.

I have learned to say *however.*

We looked in shop windows. Helen explained about Cape May diamonds. I bought a newspaper and a pound of *Laura*'s fudge. Helen, barefooted, the hem of her skirt damp, moved like the queen of a carnival. People looked at her; I am sure they were admiring her.

I suppose every man likes to have the woman he walks with admired.

"You are hardly Miss Victoria," I said.

Helen said, "I am Miss Victoria."

I want Ernie to be attracted to Anita. That is what I'm wanting.

For a while we watched a man at the convention hall steps make a profile in charcoal of a beautiful girl. His audience was quiet, only occasionally whispering to one another, like people in a cathedral.

I am not sure why I keep thinking of cathedrals.

Two or three times the girl giggled, and then her face went back to being a mask. The man was very good. The drawing did not look particularly like the girl, but it was a handsome picture.

Helen said behind her hand, "It looks the way the girl will look, someday."

The man studied his picture for almost a minute before he placed it in a cardboard frame and handed it to the girl, who was suddenly overcome with laughter. The man wore a corduroy cap. His hand trembled.

I've kept wondering how he spends his days.

I have imagined his going totally deaf.

I said, "Five minutes. Two dollars and a half. That's what the sign says. What can we lose? I wish you'd have your picture done, bare feet and all." I was not being unserious.

"The idea, Ben. Nobody should have her picture made after she is . . . older."

Another girl sat beside the easel. She could have been the first girl.

The twins' friends all look like one another.

We walked back, clear to the fishing jetty beyond our beach, and back again to our cottage. Beyond the jetty there was no sunset to speak of. The light in the sky was going, that was all.

"Generally we have sunsets," Helen said. "I remember sunsets."

I said, "We must get in the car and measure how far we've walked."

Helen said, "Of course not." She was trembling.

"All right. Of course not."

We could have been any man and woman in a beach cottage, on a cool evening, on vacation, sunburned, tired. I suppose even the most flamboyant affair turns domestic. I wondered why a man, Ernie for instance, kept, keeps playing at marriage. Or maybe marriage is playing at an affair.

The woman called from the kitchen. "I guess we're too late for the news."

The man sat with a drink. He was reading of violences, not trying to comprehend them. "I guess so."

"I think we're about ready. If you'll pour the wine."

It was an adequate meal. The man complimented the meal. The steak was just right, he said, even though it was too well done for his taste. There was an extravagant salad. He liked asparagus. He wondered why they didn't have asparagus at home more often. The rolls were perfect.

"Just heat and serve," the woman said apologetically.

The man said, "Delicious."

"What is tonight? I guess there isn't anything on television. Just reruns."

"I'll do the dishes. You're on vacation."

"Later. They'll wait. I have coffee on. We'll have coffee in the living room. We'll do the dishes later."

Under the bridge lamp Helen's hair glowed.

The man said, "You have the most beautiful hair I've ever seen."

The woman said, without looking up from the newspaper, without touching her hair, "I dye it. It used to be this color, however. I am grateful for science."

Anita, the man's wife, says, "A wash. I just use a wash."

The man is reading a news story. Again he is not attentive to what he reads. Somebody has been suspected. Someone is lying. One of the testimonies is a lie. Or perhaps no one knows the truth. Perhaps there isn't any truth to tell.

Helen said, "Cape May has a poise about it."

I said, "The widows' walks are covered and the captains' walks are uncovered. That's right, isn't it?"

"That's right. And the cupolas are merely decoration. Mama said you were carpetbaggers in Cape May until you'd been here for four generations. I'm a carpetbagger. I wouldn't dare to think what you are."

I said, "Did you ever play Cross Questions and Crooked Answers? Once I had a Sunday school teacher—it was her favorite game. She almost couldn't stand it, she thought it was so funny."

Helen said, "Who doesn't still?" She dropped her newspaper. I had folded mine. I felt prissy.

Helen said, "And tell me what was Washington like today?"

"We made grants for lectures and educational television programs and movies. We talked about justice and public opinion."

69

"That's important to you, isn't it, Ben? It's important to me, too. Generally. I'm sure I have a very good public-opinion rating."

"I told you. We said *input, output, thrust, flow,* and *point in time.*" We were looking at each other. I was determined not to drop my eyes. "We said *climax.* We said *right* to each other."

"Do they know that all the words are about . . . making love? Having sex?"

"I don't know."

"Or maybe everything is . . . sexual. I'm not abnormal, am I? Mama would die. I'd die. I want a good public-opinion rating. We all do. Maybe everybody does. We make everything difficult for each other. And I don't want to pay too much for the rating."

I said, "And then we went out to dinner together, the whole committee. And we drank too much. The steak cost a small fortune."

"And you're back at the hotel. And maybe you'll have a girl."

"Maybe. Maybe some of us will. Some of them."

"I suppose you've had a lot of girls."

"Not a lot. No. I haven't been asking you. I've deliberately not asked you. I told you I was jealous. Do you think that's funny?"

"Not funny, Ben, not at all funny. We ought to be feeling close to each other. We've been one person. It was lovely. Are you feeling close to me, Ben?"

I could have got up from the chair. I could have gone to her. When I was a kid I read a book that said, "I stopped her mouth with a kiss." I didn't understand what the book was about, but the sentence excited me. "I could barely contain my excitement," the book said. It was a Victorian book.

Helen said, "I'm feeling close to you. If I'm not, Ben, I can't stand it."

I didn't feel anything.

I imagine I have always been frightened of feeling.

A man can live a long time with a tape recording for a mind.

Helen stood. "You have to call Anita. We have to call her."

"I told you. I generally don't call on short trips. Anita has her economies. She says, 'Call if anything's not good.'"

"You didn't tell me."

"Did the subject come up?"

"The girls will want to wish you a happy Father's Day."

I did not want Anita and the girls to enter the cottage.

"Anita's even against Mother's Day. Anita says every day is Mother's Day, and Father's Day, and Children's Day."

"Easter and the Fourth of July." Helen's voice was not unkind.

I said, "You're being unkind."

"I don't mean to be. But the girls gave her an electric yogurt maker for Mother's Day. She was pleased with it."

"Anita is big on yogurt."

"I'm not being unkind. Maybe I'm in love with Anita, too."

"She has many friends, lady friends. I've never wondered about them. Not ever." I was angry.

Helen said, "I'm not lesbian. I've never been. I might be glad to be, if the occasion arose. I wait for occasions, Ben. The occasion has never arisen. You're an occasion, Ben."

I said, "I'm shocked."

"I am, too, probably. Maybe I think you're not listening."

My life has been easy. My life has been too easy.

Perhaps I am in love with Ernie.

I said, "Okay, we'll call. I'll say you weren't feeling well. I drove you on down here. I'll say the place is so beautiful that I just stayed. I'll describe the guest room. I'll describe the ocean. Anita will say, 'Good. Beautiful.'"

"Don't say I'm sick. I'm fine. I'm just marvelous."

Helen was still barefooted. She turned out the lights in the living room, in the dining room. I was following her. She stood by the kitchen light switch. She said, "There's no need, is there? You can see all right, can't you? There's still enough light to see by."

I dialed the operator. I gave my credit card number. "There's no need," Helen said.

Anita's voice spilled into the telephone. "How fine, Ben. Beautiful. I'm so glad, Ben."

Helen stood close against me. She was running her hands under my shirt.

She moved her hands down.

Her hands are strong, and efficient. *Deft*. That is a good word.

"The girls were wonderful in the recital yesterday afternoon. The Redmons' house was full, living room and dining room, even the hall, and you know how big the house is. Mrs. Wells was beside

71

herself. And the girls looked beautiful. They wore those blue dresses, the chiffon. Margot is about to outgrow hers. They got more applause than anybody. They kept saying they were too old to be in a recital—you know how they are. But they're pleased now. It was a lovely duet; they didn't miss a note. I'm glad I encouraged them."

"Slowly. Very slowly," Helen said against my ear.

I did not think of telling her to stop.

"And how do you like the cottage? Is it cold? It's turned quite cool here."

"Too. Here, too. And it's a great cottage. You'd like it. You'll like it."

"Mrs. Dodd called. They were having sudden company from Topeka. I went to dinner. Ernie was my date."

I managed to say, "Say hello to Ernie for me. I'll be home—"

"Please don't hurry. I drove Karen to Lancaster yesterday. She had an eye appointment. And Aunt Della comes tomorrow. I'm picking her up in Columbus. I told you you needed a vacation. We're getting along just fine. And the Washington business doesn't matter. You mustn't feel guilty over missing it."

"Are the girls there?" It was all I could do to talk. "I wanted to wish them happy Father's Day."

"How terrible of me. I'd forgot. Happy Father's Day. They're with Deedee. They've gone to a movie, a Disney something. It's beautiful they still like Disney things."

I wore only my shirt.

I am writing this delicately. Goddamn it. I am incapable of calling a spade a spade.

I have never been so excited in my life.

"Is Helen close by? Let me say hello."

"She's here. Here she is."

Helen held the receiver away from her ear. I undressed her slowly. She moved the receiver from her left ear to her right.

Anita said, "It's so good to hear you both. Make Ben stay. He needs an ocean. I told him. He loves the ocean."

"He's been such a help. It's hard to decide what to do about this place. I love it. We'll be talking to Mr. Kimberly. We've had supper. We've just had supper. And a long walk on the beach." Helen's voice was not breathless.

"I wish I were there."

"We do too." Helen was naked. She did not pretend to cover herself. She smiled at me. She did not look like herself. Or perhaps she looked exactly like herself, the way she was looking when she studied the charcoal picture of the girl on the boardwalk. "It's lovely here. It's really lovely. It's almost the way I remember it." She backed herself against me.

"I know it must be."

"You must come. You and the girls must come before fall. I'm sure I'll keep the place that long at least. Promise. Come. Come. Here's Ben."

I was in her. She was leaning over the kitchen table, her head in her arms.

We were having sex slowly.

"It's good to talk to you. My love to the girls. It's a great place."

Helen was coming.

I wanted to laugh.

Anita said, "I love you."

I said, "I love you, too," as I have always said.

"You mustn't run up Helen's bill. I'm glad you called."

"It's our bill. I used the card charge. I mean the charge card." I was angry for being awkward.

"Our bill then, Funny. I love you. Your number? Helen's number? I don't have it."

Helen turned to read me the number from the body of the telephone. She whispered the figures to me.

I repeated the figures. "I love you, too." All of the compartments were separate. But they fitted nicely together.

"Good night, dear. Sleep well. Promise you won't hurry. Get your visit out."

My God, that is exactly what she said.

I did not hurry.

Finally we were in Helen's poster bed. I was whispering to her. I said, "I could have written out Anita's conversation. I know the turn of her mind."

"Poor Ben," Helen said. She was asleep.

I moved away from her. I turned on the little radio by the bed.

"Clear tomorrow," a man said from Atlantic City. "In the low eighties. Good going. Good going, man."

I laughed with the man. I got up and opened the drapes. I didn't want to go to sleep. I wanted to stay awake forever. I got back in bed. I pressed myself against Helen. The sea was loud.

"Yes, yes," Helen said in her sleep. The radio played "In the Still of the Night."

I dreamed of my father. I thought, "I am dreaming of my father, and I can't remember what I am dreaming."

I do not believe, "Like father, like son." I do not believe, "As the twig is bent." I do not believe, "Whatsoever a man sows." I do not believe any of the easy sayings.

And I do not know difficult sayings.

Or all of the sayings are too difficult for saying.

I was cold. The radio said, "It's fifty-one degrees out there. They missed again. Showers. Scattered showers. Get out your umbrella again, buddy." Surely it was not the same man who had said, "You just heard 'In the Still of the Night.' How did you like 'The Still of the Night'? Be still, man. Be still in the night."

"Be still," Helen said. She was over me. "How good this is."

"Good." My mouth was dry. "Let me brush my teeth. Let me get up."

"You're up, Ben. No. I want you to be dirty, Ben. Yes, Ben. Nice and dirty. Yes, yes."

Rain fell against the windows.

I thought about Ernie.

I wished I had somebody to tell about Helen.

There wasn't anybody to tell. There would never be anybody. *Lonely* means not having anybody to tell anything. A man needs to be involved in the world. I am not involved. I am a tape recorder.

Someday, I thought, if Helen and I got to be old people on a summer beach, I could not say, "Do you remember that Sunday morning, Helen? Do you remember what we were doing?" I thought, "You're a dumb bastard; you think like a dumb bastard."

Helen said, "Happy Father's Day."

"I'm not your father."

"That's nice, too. It's nice not to be afraid of getting pregnant. I used to wake sometimes, just paralyzed, absolutely paralyzed with fear. There are advantages. There are always advantages."

I said, "That's what Anita says. She'll be glad when she doesn't have to be afraid." I heard what I said after I had said it.

But it was all right. Helen said, "It's nice for you to talk about Anita. It's lovely. Anita is my good friend. Everything is lovely."

I relish the act of sex. Perhaps, even more, I relish the moment after the moment. That's what I was saying to myself. I said, "Maybe I've never had a nice girl before."

"Anita's nice."

"Yes."

"You'll tell me. You'll tell me about the others." She pressed closer against me.

It pleases me to think that one human body can always press closer to another human body.

I forget to be pleased with such knowledge.

Helen said, "What is the most unlikely thing we could do today?"

"Tell you about the others, the few others. Get up and put on our bathing suits and go swimming in the cold rain. Call all the Kimberlys to come to breakfast, all six, seven, eight of them. Shoot sea gulls with a cannon."

"Pull up the covers, Ben. I'm cold. There aren't many birds, are there, not like on other beaches? And it's not a good shell beach. Mama always said that; even Mama admitted that."

"Cape May is my favorite beach."

"The rain's slackening."

"Should we get dressed?"

"Listen. Wait a minute."

"It's harder again."

"It will rain all day. It will rain forever."

"No it won't, no matter how much I wish it would."

We were together. I do not know which of us said which sentences. That is what I am meaning about the moment after.

75

Helen said, "The service is at eleven. That's what the lady said. We don't want to be late." I didn't know what she was talking about. "You used to have to cover your arms at St. Mark's, even your arms, a long time ago. You had to buy paper sleeves. You don't have to any more, not even cover your head. I don't own a hat. But I'll wear a long-sleeved dress, the green suit, the one with the embroidered henna roses. Do you know what color henna is, Ben? It's an old-fashioned color. I bought a lot of clothes to come to Athens. I wanted to impress somebody. I'm always hoping to impress somebody."

I said, "Impress. Everybody knows what henna means." I sat up. "You're fooling. You're making a joke."

"I like to think about going to church with you."

"Cut it out, Helen."

"Don't you go to church?"

"Sometimes. Sure. I'm big at Christmas and funerals, and when the girls sing in choruses. I go. Hell, yes I go. Everybody is old enough to go to funerals and choruses. You're pulling my leg."

I suppose many men become angry remembering religion.

My religion lasted until I was fourteen years old.

"I'm doing that, too. I'm pulling your leg, Ben. Lovely. It's still lovely."

"What are you? Some kind of religious nut?"

"They have two thousand seats. Nobody will notice us. I want to do things we can't imagine doing."

"We have. We are."

The tabernacle was like a basketball stadium, a vast concrete building. I imagined the girls leading cheers. The chairs were funeral-parlor chairs.

We did not look very different from the other people. I suppose I was expecting the kind of crowd that used to attend the tent-meeting revivals on East State Street. My father raised hell with me for going. I went with somebody named F. O. Baker. "You're an Episcopalian, Ben, and don't you forget it. F. O.'s a bad influence."

I don't suppose my father ever stepped inside the church: he was rolled in for his funeral. But the church was as important to him as my making *A*'s or taking dancing lessons or being an Eagle Scout or saying *sir* and *ma'am*. "Church, home, state, in that order," my father said. "That's what being an American means, goddamn it, and you're not going to forget it."

We were late. Helen had forgotten her white gloves and purse. She had to look for them. She found them in her little bathroom. "Nobody goes without white gloves," Helen kept saying. Anita wears white gloves to lectures and church. But Anita has never had to hunt for anything. She has always known where to go back to.

We sat alone in the last row of the funeral chairs. I was sorry Helen, in her green suit, had not moved into the crowd of worshipers. We were twenty empty rows behind anybody else. I felt exposed, envying the community of the believers, I suppose, with their placards that told their brotherhood: Afghanistan, USA—Hawaii had a separate sign—Spain, Ireland, Canada; I tried to locate Helen's Baptist lady.

We were younger, perhaps a little younger, than most of the people. But there were children present. Far up on our right three young couples sat sedately together, muscular and browned. I imagined them on beds, naked. Cape May is a family beach.

On the flag-draped stage, behind a pulpit, a fat lady in a blue dress sang "The Beatitudes." She had a good enough voice. She was accompanied on a piano by a fat lady in pink. There were flowers on a table below the stage: stock, Fiji mums, carnations— florist flowers. It was strange to have florist flowers in June. Perhaps the flowers were plastic.

A blue velvet curtain hung across the back of the stage. Three lines of silver letters hung on the curtain. The curtain swayed a little, as rocking chairs sway on a windy porch. The words were hard to read.

I memorized the words while a man read Scripture and another man prayed.

> WORTHY IS THE LAMB THAT WAS SLAIN
> TO RECEIVE POWER, AND RICHES, AND WISDOM, AND
> STRENGTH, AND HONOR, AND GLORY, AND BLESSING.

A silver globe, swaying, hung under the words. I could make out the East Coast of the United States. The words were crazily spaced. I kept thinking I would use the words sometime. At a dinner party I would turn to the woman on my left, or I would get the attention of the whole group. "WORTHY IS THE LAMB THAT WAS SLAIN," I would shout, "TO RECEIVE POWER, AND SUCCESS, AND WISDOM AND—" I was saying the words wrong. I had left out RICHES. Over and over I practiced the words. I couldn't imagine what they meant.

The woman beside me, Anita, or Helen, or some person without a face would say, "Of course, Ben. Why, of course."

There was a collection. The pink fat lady played a passage from *Humoresque,* with many extra trills. The usher was black. Some of the dark ladies in the audience wore saris. The black usher smiled. His smile was pasted on his face. I tossed a five-dollar bill into the collection plate. The twins' picture glared at me. Helen smiled. I pressed my leg against hers.

One man introduced another man. The other man introduced an Indian. The Baptist lady was wrong: he wasn't from South America. The three men welcomed us again to the Global Congress of Christians. The Indian said, "We represent twenty-seven countries." I thought, "Not counting Indianapolis and Athens, Ohio." I thought, "You are smartass, Ben Adams. You are very smartassed."

I do not know how many countries inhabit the globe.

The Indian was speaking against the World Council of Churches. The audience was responsive. Several times they laughed happily, like a recording of laughter on a television comedy. The man was evidently making jokes. It was good to sit beside Helen. She was listening to what the man said, as if he spoke importantly. I did not mind attending the tabernacle.

I was conscious of Helen's breathing. I matched my breathing to hers. Her breath was slow and long. Anita breathes more quickly. I am used to Anita's breath. I tried to think about Anita. I tried to feel guilty.

I wished Anita blessings. I did not have anything to think about her.

The Indian was saying, "God is not only God of the infinite, but of the infinitesimal," which wasn't a bad idea. He said, "One with the Lord is a majority." He said, "God can do anything but fail."

I cannot remember feeling more detached. The church was full of people's backs. Perhaps the people wore no faces at all. Perhaps the backs of the people in the church were the only faces left on the globe.

Had they all begun to cohabit, or turn into trees, or disappear, I would not have been surprised.

I touched my face. I looked at Helen. Helen wore her listening face. Her face was worn.

The Indian said, "The dimensions of the universe." He said, "Love." He was saying something about love.

I thought love, which is fuck, which is everything, which is nothing, which is love. I thought Vaseline, Italy, Orangutang.

They sang a hymn. Helen and I held a hymnal together. She sang softly. I did not pretend to sing.

We left by the side door we had come in by. I touched Helen's arm, leading her. She did not pull back.

I said, "A man and a woman should probably go to church together."

I did not start the car immediately. We had left the windows closed. The car was warm.

Helen said, "I didn't see the Baptist lady, did you? I was looking for her. I saw the Canada standard, however. Evidently there aren't many people from Canada."

"I didn't see her. They have a small population."

"I would have liked to have talked to her, to talk to some of the people. They looked so dedicated. You could tell they cared terribly about what the man said."

I said, "He seemed more against than for." I did not want to hurt her feelings. Perhaps the service had meant something to her.

"Thank you for going. It wasn't much, I suppose. But it was something different. You're right. It's good for a man and a woman to go to church together.

"It was interesting. That fellow had a pleasing voice."

I should have said something that sounded important. I imagined then, I imagine even now, that the minute was important, the two of us sitting in the car together. I can't imagine what either of us could have said to the other. But it is good for a man and a woman, having made love, to have sat next to each other while somebody spoke of possibilities, the eternal, and the sacred.

79

I started the engine. Helen lowered her window. "Turn right. We need to go to the grocery again. I meant to get ice cream last night. It's a special. I saw it advertised on the window. We're having raspberries and ice cream for dessert."

Again I was a youngish man, feeling young on a holiday; again Helen and I played a little domestic scene.

"Thank you, Mrs. Adams."

"My pleasure, Mr. Adams."

She chose a half dozen items.

The girl at the checkout counter recognized Helen. "How are you?" they asked each other. They told each other it would probably turn out to be a good day. The girl was pretty. She wore gold earrings. "Your coupon, ma'am? For the ice cream?"

"I didn't know. Where do you get them?"

"We had a circular. And there's an ad in the Philadelphia *Inquirer*."

"I'll just buy an *Inquirer* then. I noticed a machine out front, Ben. You don't mind, do you?"

Fortunately, nobody waited behind us in line. If Anita had asked me to leave a store to buy a newspaper for a coupon to save twenty cents on ice cream . . . But Anita wouldn't have asked me. She carries a little leather case for coupons.

When I came back there were two people behind Helen. "I insist," Helen kept saying. "You go right ahead." She and the clerk, laughing, moved our packages. Helen took the fat newspaper to an empty lane. She spread the paper out on the counter in front of her. She was laughing. "You think I'm crazy, don't you?"

"Absolutely. Don't stop to read the news stories."

"I'm not. I'm absolutely not."

I was laughing, too.

"I don't like ice cream much. And I never save coupons."

I said, "Today we are doing things we can't imagine doing. That's what you said."

"And this. I'll pick day-lily buds from the backyard. I've always wanted to eat day lilies. I've read about them."

"You come back soon," the girl said.

The people in the line were laughing with us.

I remember laughing as a child. Sometimes I kept laughing after I had stopped being amused.

We picked day-lily buds.

The sky was gray.

"Twins," Helen said.

I kept laughing after I had stopped being amused.

I do not think of myself as an anxious man. Anita is anxious, she says she is. "If I didn't keep busy I would worry myself to death," she says. "The children, our health, the country, bombs and pollution. But worry is a sin, really and truly. *Reely.*" Anita says *reely* when she is making commandments. Sometimes she annoys me. She winks when she says *reely.* Anita makes up commandments as she lives along, adjusting them to the occasion, obeying the commandment before it is uttered, living, thus, a totally righteous life. "It's a sin to spend money just for the sake of spending," and, "It's a sin not to buy at least four *reely* nice outfits for all of us every year." It's wrong to coddle the children, and it's wrong not to coddle them, everybody needs a little coddling; and they reely need new horses. It's a sin to . . .

After a fashion, it is my reasoning. I am being unfair.

I am anxious. Everybody who keeps living one day after another must surely think himself righteous, even a man who, say, kills.

While Helen cooked lunch-dinner, I read at the *Inquirer.* I turned on the television set, a cable channel. Supermarket music played in the background while dials flipped announcing the winds, the humidity, the temperature of the land, of the sea. A voice came over the music and the circles. It was June, with storm warnings in the Midwest, freezing in Seattle, a heat wave in Texas. Bridges fell, ships sank, boilers exploded, Anita died, the girls, Helen's fires and floods raced over Cape May and Athens, Ohio.

I am a goddamned fool. Again I thought of gathering all of the world that mattered to me into a plane: the people who matter, I am not saying the people I love; I do not know about love. I am an aged Catcher in the Rye.

I would fly them to a place where the sun shone and the air was

81

good. I would fly them to June, the weather I expect June to be. Perhaps I am talking about love.

It would be a vast plane. I would include more then my family— Helen, of course, Ernie and the ladies in the office, even the people with faces I cannot imagine when their backs are turned, the fat lady who sang "The Beatitudes."

The plane fell. The plane always fell. I was always on the plane, too. I could see the backs of the passengers, almost all of the passengers.

I threw the newspaper down. I picked it up and folded it. I called, "When's soup on?" I have never said "When's soup on?" in my life. I pushed myself up from the chair.

"A little while yet." Helen stood at the kitchen sink. She was perspiring. "I know you must be starved. I'm being terribly clumsy. I've burned the carrots. I'm working at burning the flounder."

"I have a taste for burned flounder. Can't I do something?"

"Don't watch me, Ben. Please." Helen put her hand to her mouth.

"You shouldn't be bothering. I told you."

"I want to. Please."

I went back to the living room.

"You're not annoyed, are you?" Helen called.

"Of course not. The very idea."

"Your music sounds nice. Turn it up a little, won't you?" I turned up my music. "Or take a walk. Take a little walk, just a little one," Helen shouted over the music. "Not long."

I thought of going into the kitchen to kiss her good-bye, but I didn't. I closed the screen door quietly, as if someone slept, or as if I left a funeral parlor.

There was a thin place in the clouds. I assumed the sun was behind it.

I walked the boardwalk to the fishermen's jetty. The beach was crowded. The fringes of the colored umbrellas flapped in the wind. As I watched, a green and white umbrella fell. It scooted a little

82

way, to be stopped by a neighbor's island of umbrella and chairs. It was only an umbrella's falling; it was not a plane. But the people were disturbed. A child cried. I could not hear the child over the waves. I did not stop to watch. The umbrella and the people moved no faster than figures in a series of drawings.

I am not a mystic.

I do not have the slightest patience with Anita, for instance, when she says, "I just knew that was going to happen." When we married, Anita was always feeling something in her bones. We had our first argument over the feeling in her bones. "Very well," Anita said, "I won't mention it anymore, but you can't control the feeling in my bones." Of course, she has mentioned it regularly. I have stopped remonstrating.

At the beach with Helen, I was surprised at how often I remembered when I was young. I disapprove of men and women who say, "When I was twelve, when I was eight, when I was fourteen." At parties I have said, "A human being has enough going for him now without dragging in twelve, eight, fourteen. Or against him." Anita says, "That's the kind of thing Ben likes to say." We smile at each other.

When I was young, I was often alone. My father came home from his office on Court Street at eight o'clock; we had supper at eight-fifteen. Always the cooks, housekeepers, mistresses—whatever they were—shopped, visited friends, talked on the telephone. I did not mind being alone, back in those presocial days, back before dinner parties. I read all of the science fiction books in the county library and at the university. I was proud of my university card. My father got it for me.

I hope Mrs. Phalp was my father's mistress. I have never said to myself before, "I hope Mrs. Phalp slept with my father."

I do not know why I have been reticent to myself.

When I imagined they were together, I turned my radio loud. I locked the door to my room.

I am interested in my sense of morality. I do not think my morality is merely a matter of living from one day through the next.

Mrs. Phalp was always feeling something in her bones. I have never mentioned Mrs. Phalp to Anita. "I don't care," Mrs. Phalp said. "There's really something to it."

I practiced feeling in my bones. "The telephone is going to ring, Mrs. Phalp." Sometimes it did. "It's going to be Mrs. Hathaway." Sometimes it was. The telephone was always ringing; Mrs. Hathaway was Mrs. Phalp's best friend. Mr. Hathaway ran the grocery store. across the street. I remember the grocery well. I wish I could remember the apartment Mrs. Phalp and my father and I lived in.

"You do beat all," Mrs. Phalp said, and I felt proud.

When she went to the hospital I said to myself, "Mrs. Phalp is going to die."

She died. I think she loved my father. I would like to think that somebody loved my father.

"A child is ridiculously impressionable." That's what Anita likes to say. I was impressionable. I should have told Anita about Mrs. Phalp and the ringing telephones. On the boardwalk I remembered Mrs. Phalp as the umbrella scooted. I said to myself, "I did not know the umbrella was going to fall."

I have never honestly known when anything was going to happen.

I was at the Sea Gull, the motel on our left. I began to run. It was raining. I would have run to get out of the rain anyhow.

Helen stood in the dining room doorway. She held the telephone receiver. "Anita, how marvelous. How good it is to hear you. Ben's coming in the door, this minute. How's that for timing? He's been for a walk. It's raining, wouldn't you know it? It's so nice to hear you. Wait, I want to talk to you. But here. Here's Ben, first."

I took the receiver from her. Our hands did not touch. I had no reason to be frightened of what Helen might say to Anita. We were grown people, not twelve, or eight, or fourteen.

"Are you all right? The girls all right?"

"You sound breathless. Of course we're all right. You're all right?"

"Just great. Helen's cooking dinner. She's burned the carrots."

"Ben, don't tease." Anita has a high laugh. "I'm sure she hasn't."

Helen took the receiver from me. Our hands did not touch. "He's not teasing. I keep thinking about the good meals at your house. I'm starving him to death. But I like to cook. I want to be able to cook. The sea air is good for him. We got some sun yesterday. You're nice to lend him to me."

I took the receiver. "What are you up to?"

"I wanted to hear your voices, that's mostly why. I needn't have called. But sometimes you act silly if I don't mention things."

When people have been married a long time, secrets are *from* instead of *with* each other.

"What? What's the matter?" I pressed the receiver hard against my ear. I did not want Helen to listen.

"It's Aunt Della. She wants me to drive her to Lexington, where she was born. She's taken a sudden notion. She's not well, Ben."

Anita's voice dropped.

"What? I can't hear you."

"She's failed," Anita whispered. "She's failed terribly. She's not herself."

I thought of saying, "That's good. That would be a turn for the better." On the beach with Helen I had learned to use my joking voice. Perhaps that is the voice I use for the twins. I made up my voice for Mrs. Phalp a long time ago.

Anita said, "She thinks she's going to die. She wants to die in Lexington. She wants to be cremated. She wants me to hire a helicopter and sprinkle her ashes over Lexington. We're leaving about three."

"My lord. I'll be home."

"What's the matter?" Helen reached for the telephone, but I turned my back to her.

"Please don't come."

"Don't be silly. I can get a plane this afternoon, a bus, something. I'm coming."

"Ben, really, I'm insisting. Ernie just dropped by. He said he needed to go to Lexington, on that Paul Kendall deal. He says everything is fine at the office. Janice adores to be in charge. He said it was a kindness to Janice. He insists on going with us."

Everybody in the wide green world insists.

Anita coughed. "And I'm probably exaggerating about Aunt Della. She's probably all right. And Ernie wants to go with us."

The receiver hurt my ear.

Anita enjoys crises as much as she enjoys challenges. Perhaps the words are the same. Her voice was ragged, or brave. "I'm taking the girls, of course. They don't want to go, but they'll have a good time. They can swim and ride with Ransom's girls. And promise me you won't hurry home. Let me be on my own. Let me handle things."

I couldn't remember Ransom. She is evidently one of the women who visit us. Evidently she boasts of girls. I said, "I want to."

"No, I insist. Promise me. Please, Ben."

With tears in her voice, Anita has said, "Promise me. Promise me you'll buy a new suit."

Aunt Della died. Last night I learned that Aunt Della had died. She carried her will in her purse.

It is wrong to try to wallow in guilt. That is one of the commandments, one of the million commandments. It is lying. Guilt is having it both ways: you do what you want to do, and you pretend otherwise. The *otherwise* makes up for the joy of indulgence. My God, we all even out.

Anita said, "I want to be here when you get home. Surely the weather will change. It's cold and rainy here too." Always we give each other weather reports on the telephone. Anita's voice was happy.

I said, "It got down to forty-eight last night."

"My goodness. Oh, happy Father's Day again. The girls are at the club. They send you their love. I'm not sorry I called. I'm glad I called, if you promise not to rush home. Promise?"

"I'm full of promises. The same to you."

"Let me say good-bye to Helen."

I handed the receiver to Helen, not wanting to. I had never thought about the word *receiver* before.

Helen held the receiver away from her ear. Anita's voice crackled in the air between us. "I wanted you to know. We found your bracelet, the stunning silver one. I forgot to tell you last night. Mrs. Michaels found it. You must have been frantic."

"How nice. I hadn't missed it. We've been so busy. I'm afraid I'm a terribly careless woman. When you get down to it, I'm a mess."

"You're nothing of the kind. We'll mail it. And thanks again for taking such good care of Ben. I know he's having a beautiful time. I can tell by his voice."

"Don't worry about the bracelet. I'm very well fixed."

I reached for the receiver.

Helen shifted it to her other ear.

Helen said, "I'll send him home in good shape, shaped up. Don't you worry about him."

"I'm not worrying. But Aunt Della."

Helen and I listened in detail to Anita's telling again about Aunt Della. "Ashes, Helen. Imagine! Ashes!"

"Poor darling," Helen said, "I know what you're going through."

"I know you do. You know better than anybody. You are why I called. I wanted to talk to Ben, too, of course. Tell him happy Father's Day again. I'm not really upset, not *reely*." Anita's voice was jolly again. She wanted Helen to know how much she loved the hot tray. Nobody had ever had a nicer hostess gift. Anita didn't know how she had got along without it, all these years.

I thought of Mrs. Phalp and Mrs. Hathaway. I am astounded at how much people find to say to each other on telephones.

I was glad Anita was, or posed as, a contented wife and mother, inhabiting a globe.

I had meant to pretend to tell this story in a straight line. I know that life does not happen in a straight line. Life crisscrosses and dovetails and goes back as much as forward.

I am a goddamned philosopher.

I am making a big goddamned deal.

87

Anita's stories turn out happily. The bracelets or contact lenses get found; the tree isn't really struck by lightning, just the clothespole; the skin disease is only a rash and goes away.

Aunt Della's death was a happy ending. "We were in the doctor's office. She just passed away. She just passed. Over. She wanted to go. I'm not sad, Ben."

Helen's stories do not end unhappily. They are only the beginnings of stories.

I suppose I do not tell stories.

I am happier because Anita's stories end happily.

On the telephone Helen said to Anita, "And *thank you. Thank you again.*" She spoke as if she hit each word.

Helen fitted the receiver into the cradle. "She said to tell you not to hurry home. She said to tell you again."

I said, "Good. I can't stay forever, though, no matter how nice it's been."

"I know. She said she liked to think of her husband's being happy with one of her best friends. Anita has many friends, doesn't she? Have you been happy with many of them?"

"We're both voyeurs, aren't we?" I did not want to talk to Helen. "I suppose so."

"I envy people with many best friends. And it was certainly different from last night, wasn't it? The telephone conversation, I mean." She moved back from me. I was not going to reach for her, but I was annoyed with her for moving away.

"Yes, I guess it was different. You can't have sex twenty-four hours a day. I can't."

"You do pretty well. And there, for a minute, you were afraid of what I was going to say."

"Of course I wasn't. Something smells good in there."

"It's the flounder. The burning flounder."

In the kitchen I stood behind Helen. I did not want her to know I was excited again.

We should have quarreled then and had it over.

I am used to Anita. Anita and I are probably wrong. I have said, too, "Anything but a quarrel."

If Anita and I had fought more, if we had brought our pettinesses and prejudices into the open . . .

We would have been the same. I am probably glad we have not quarreled.

Once Tina said, "You and Daddy don't fuss together, not the way other girls' parents do, Deedee's parents. I wish somebody would fight over us."

Anita said, "What a lovely thing for a daughter to say. We're both standing up for you. We're a family. Isn't that lovely to think about?" Anita was crying.

We were at dinner; we were arguing; Anita calls an argument a discussion. The girls wanted to go to an all-night movie, or they wanted to give up their bras: "Nobody else wears them." The girls need brassieres. Sometimes I am embarrassed, looking at them. They are women. When they walk across a room they turn imaginary corners. I am embarrassed that I am embarrassed.

Or they wanted to dye their hair.

Anita said, "We are of a mind. Your father and I agree."

Margot said, "I wish to hell you wouldn't say that."

Anita put down her fork. "We will not have that kind of language in our house, at our dinner table, Margot."

"I'm sorry," Margot said. "Forgive me."

I was sorry Margot said, "I'm sorry."

Helen and I barely talked through dinner. Braised, the lily buds tasted like the asparagus. Anita never serves the same vegetables two days straight. The flounder could have been anything, leather, paper, clothing. I complimented the raspberries and ice cream.

We did the dishes together. Helen began chattering; she was making conversation: she didn't recognize any of the dishes, or the silver either, she wondered where on earth Mr. Kimberly had found such tacky stuff; Mama didn't approve of dishwashers; Mama had never lived in a house, even an apartment, with a dishwasher; the weather was absolutely impossible; she felt particularly sorry for the little secretaries who slaved in offices and looked forward to a weekend, and what did they have? fog and rain, and more rain; it was going to rain all afternoon, cats and dogs.

I said, "I wish to hell you wouldn't say that."

89

"Say what?"

"What you've been saying. The conversation."

She put her arms around me.

We went upstairs to her bedroom. There was only anger in our sex.

It was like fighting. We were daring each other and taking each other's dare. We bit and clawed.

I grabbed the hair of her head. I pulled her head back, almost to her shoulders.

Helen called out all the words we had both pretended we were too delicate to say.

I called them back to her.

I am grateful for words.

I am grateful for every word.

Perhaps an orgy excludes tenderness. The other times we had pretended tenderness.

Here, in this cabin, I do not care.

"Say what? What was I saying wrong?" Helen asked when we had satisfied each other. She lay in my arms.

"What you said. While we were doing the dishes. You were furious with Anita, weren't you?"

"Well, listen to Mr. Smart who reads minds. Just listen to him. Why didn't you tell me then what I was thinking? You had time, Mr. Smart Shit. I don't mean to say that, excuse me. I mean Mr. Smart."

"I'm your guest." I do not like to remember my logic any more than my anger. I was not loving Anita. I was not even wanting to defend her. I was hating Helen with completeness I had not known I could feel. "You were making fun of her. You were telling her we'd slept together."

She did not pull away from me. Instead she began caressing me.

Even if I live to be an old man I will remember Helen's mouth and hands.

90   Helen said, "I wouldn't tell her for anything, not for my life, even though she should be told."

I said, "We have a splendid secret, you and I, my love, my sea gull, my—"

"Funny. Ben Adams is a very funny man. His wife has everything; she is a very funny lady. She spreads her legs and wins prizes:
children and houses and love. She feels sorry for everybody who
isn't funny Ben's wife." Helen was playing with herself.

I shifted my body. Helen's other hand followed me. I said,
"Don't."

"You love it. Big old Ben reacts and reacts. Big Ben is a master
man. He will tell everybody at the office and the country club and
the bank. Big old Ben. I don't care. But Helen won't tell." It was
hardly Helen's voice. It was Helen's voice.

I am telling.

I am typing.

I am telling somebody on Helen.

I did not push her away from me. "Goddamn you. Goddamn
you."

"Big old Ben's wife thinks I am too old to be jealous of."

I was more surprised than I had been when she shouted the obscenities, when we shouted the obscenities. "That's not fair. Stop it.
We've got to do something. I want to say something."

"I'm doing something, Big Old Ben Blubber."

I lay in the center of the globe.

"Nobody's as good as you, old Ben. The Los Angeles kid, he was
good too. He learned fast. The carryout boy at the A and P in Indianapolis. The Standard Oil man in Indianapolis, just a mile from our
house. The fellow in Florence, and the one in Malta. You'll be dead
when they're as old as you are."

I said, "My God."

Somebody in the past said, "Be sure to say your prayers, Ben
Adams."

Helen spoke carefully against me. "And when you are forty-five,
I'll be fifty-five. Happy birthday. Anita already has your present. It's
already wrapped, but she opened it to show me. You're going to
get—no, I won't spoil the surprise. But it's monogrammed, Ben, the
way you are. And when you are sixty, I will be seventy and I will be
dead. I won't be an old woman. I won't slobber and wet myself.
Ben, Ben, Ben, oh, Ben."

91

She was out of the bed. She stood naked at the dormer window that faced the brick wall of the Sea Gull. She lifted her hands and pushed back the curtains.

Rain fell.

She looked like an old woman.

That was when she said she wanted to run a motel with glass walls to make up for all the lives she couldn't live.

Helen said, "I've been cheated."

I said, "My God, Helen. Nobody tells anybody everything. Anything."

"It could be any time of day, couldn't it?" Her voice was suddenly soft. "I'm getting wet. Look, Ben."

I sat up. She turned slowly. She held her breasts in her hands. "I was slumping, wasn't I? 'Walk straight, Helen,' Mama always said. 'Hold yourself straight.' The Baptist lady complimented us. I do pretty well, don't I, don't I, Ben? When I worked, a long time ago, a very long time ago, there were opportunities. A woman runs out of opportunities. Don't I, don't I, Ben?"

I loved Helen, whatever love means.

I could not remember Helen's other voice.

Perhaps I loved myself for a minute. I think I have never known the meaning of "Love thy neighbor as thyself."

It is almost impossible to love thyself.

I am full of sayings. I have memorized many sayings. I thought of the blue fat lady singing "The Beatitudes."

"Mama always took rain hard. 'It's raining, Helen. Hurry. Close the windows. It's raining in. Run up and close the windows. Hurry!'"

"Mrs. Phalp did too."

Closing windows is an urgency for Anita.

"I'm wet, front and back."

I said her name.

"I'm not closing any of the windows, Ben."

She did not say, "I'm sorry for what we have said to each other."

Always, all of my married life, I have learned to say, "Forgive me."

Helen did not cry. I have assumed that tears were a part of argu-

92

ments, of discussions. I am unnecessarily upset by tears, even though Tina and Margot weep as a kind of conversation.

Anita administers tears.

Helen did not pick up the church clothes she had torn from herself. She stepped on the clothes. My clothes lay folded on the slipper chair. Anita has trained me well. Or perhaps I have always folded my clothes.

"Hurry, Ben, hurry," Helen had kept saying after we left the telephone.

Even at home, days pass ridiculously fast.

Even when at morning I think, "How will I get through this day?" days pass ridiculously fast.

Helen came back to the bed. She was wet with rain, and cold. She did not pretend to dry herself.

I lay on her arm.

I tried to remember a poem I had memorized a long time ago. I could not remember the poem. It was about a man who lay on a woman's arm in winter.

Helen said, "It could be almost any season of the year."

"Yes." I was kissing her throat and her breasts.

Helen said, "I know you have to go home. Everybody does who can."

Helen said, "Yes, I wanted to tell on you, on us. That wasn't very nice, was it? A lot of times I'm not very nice. I told you. I'm not bragging. I don't think people brag about not being very nice. Yes, Ben. Yes, yes, yes."

I was tired. I could not imagine making love again, but I did not stop kissing her.

"I could drive you to Atlantic City. Surely planes go from Atlantic City. Or Philadelphia, Wherever planes go from. I'd like to drive you somewhere."

"Yes, yes."

In the still room Helen said, "We could be almost any age, couldn't we?"

She settled her head on my shoulder.

I said, "This has been good. Thank you. I'm grateful to you."

93

"The thanks go the other way." Helen patted my chest. "We are writing each other bread-and-butter notes. 'Dear Anita and Ben. What a marvelous time I had at your house, your home, and afterwards. I shall treasure the memories of . . .'"

" 'Dear Helen. Let me say again what a pleasure it was for me to . . .'"

We were almost laughing.

I said, "I suppose everything's closed. The travel agencies. Sunday. I could probably get a bus to Columbus. Nothing goes to Athens. Or leaves. Athens is the center of the world."

"I could call Mr. Kimberly. He probably knows everything."

I said, "Why do you call him 'Mister'?" I was jealous of the little man who had known Helen for years. I think I am wrong. I make commandments too. I think a human being, faithless, should not expect faithfulness. I have no right to expect a final loyalty, even from Anita, or the girls. I said, "No, don't bother. I was just wondering."

"A dozen years ago, longer," Helen said. "You and I think in dozens, don't we? We are old enough to think in dozens. He was young then, and thin. At first he always called me, 'Miss Helen.' I started calling him 'Mister,' that's all. He probably pretends I don't remember what happened. He was pathetic, Ben. It's pathetic to be young, too. We've said that, haven't we?"

This typewriter can type out the word *remember* by itself.

"I know."

"Tell me something, Ben. Tell me a secret."

"There was a girl in Chicago, awhile ago. It was a convention. She was a part of the convention, an insurance convention." I did not remember the girl very well. I told what I remembered, adding a detail or two, not wanting to disappoint Helen. "She lisped. She had a tattoo on her thigh, the inside of her thigh, a little Valentine."

"Really? I'm glad," Helen said.

"Really," I said, surprised at what I was imagining, surprised that I felt the need for imagining.

"Good. Thank you. That's a nice story. She was a poor little secretary, and it rained all the time she was on vacation."

"Probably."

I did not think I was going crazy. I do not think I am going crazy. *Going* and *crazy* are interesting words.

"I can remember when there wasn't Kleenex. Once I rode in a horse and buggy to get to a farm my father owned near Indianapolis."

I said, "I remember . . ."

"Don't tell me if you can't remember. I can remember when there weren't plastic bags. For Kotex my mother tore up sheets." Her voice was hateful. "I can remember when we didn't have packaged foods, not the way we do now. We weren't packaged when I was as old as your girls."

"Come on, Helen."

"I stopped being a virgin when I was younger than your girls. He was a hired man. He was filthy. I can remember too much."

"Don't."

"And I kept on being packaged. I don't know what I'm talking about."

"No, Helen. This has been fine."

"I know what I'm talking about. What if the professional daughter loved you? What if I loved you, Ben? Among the packages. And don't laugh. It's hard for me to touch people. It's hard for women like me to touch people. When I can touch I'm saved, for a minute. I can touch you, Ben."

I was saying the words a man says when he is confronted away from the happy conventions, the packages, he lives among. I was saying, "Silly," "No," "You don't mean that."

Helen said, "Mama always said, 'How beautiful is the house of memories.' That's what she said. It's a whorehouse. I suppose I hated Mama. Does everybody hate everybody?"

I could have said, "Of course you didn't. Anita says you are the most faithful, generous . . ." I said, "Whatever hate means."

"*Whatever.* I learned to say that from you. That's right. I'm not saying, 'I love you, Ben.'"

I may as well remember it all.

The sound of a man's crying is an ugly sound.

I suppose I have not cried since my father died.

I listened to myself.

It was like the sound of a dog's barking.

Or I did not listen. I am remembering the sounds of a dog's bark. I lay alone in an apartment. Everybody in the world had left the house, all the compartments. Somewhere a dog barked.

Helen did not comfort me. If a man cried in front of Anita she would smother him with comfort. "Poor baby," Anita would say. "My darling, darling baby."

Helen did not say, "I'm sorry, Ben."

I was glad she did not cry, or touch me.

I will probably not cry again. I thought, crying, "This is the last time I will cry."

"It's just time, Ben," Helen said. I think that is what she said.

After a while we dressed. Helen put on her raincoat. I put on my new shirt and sweater.

We walked in the rain, to the east end of the beach and the west.

Only two men stood on the fishermen's jetty. They wore boots and hats.

We ate hamburgers and drank coffee at a restaurant across from the boardwalk. It was almost dark. We were the only people in the restaurant.

At home, at the cottage, we watched television for a while. It was a series about a family. I thought, even as I watched, "I am forgetting what I watch."

The weatherman said, "Rain again. I am tired of reading this report."

Helen yawned. She sat on the couch beside me, slumped. She had kicked off her shoes.

"Good night, Ben, old Ben."

"Good night, old Helen, Miss Helen."

"I'll drive you to Philadelphia tomorrow. It's a nice drive, only a couple of hours. I'm sure a lot of planes go to Columbus from Philadelphia. We'll check tomorrow."

"Or not check. We can be surprised. We've done things we've never done before."

"Nobody does anything she's never done before."

"That's silly. I'm always checking planes. For the first time. But there isn't any need."

"I want to, to drive you up."

She was standing. I stood. My foot had gone to sleep. I staggered a little. "I suppose . . ." I didn't know what I was going to say. I imagined I knew what she was going to say.

I do not believe stories about love.

I said, "I'll sleep downstairs, in my room, the room for guests."

"Good on you. All right, Ben."

We did not kiss good-night. We touched cheeks, the way a man touches cheeks with women who have been visiting his wife.

I woke early. It was not seven. I had slept well, dreaming I suppose, and forgetting my dreams. Helen was already up. She sang in the kitchen, a song I didn't know.

She surely heard me, as I heard her. I could not remember what guests do who wake in strange houses.

There was fog.

I shaved and dressed and packed before I went into the kitchen in my new shirt and sweater.

Helen was starting bacon. Scrambled eggs the color of her suit waited in a plastic bowl.

"Good morning, Ben. How nice you look."

"Good morning. How nice you look."

She looked as if she had wandered into the kitchen to pose for a picture.

I said, "I thought we'd walk on the beach. Last look."

She pushed the skillet to the back of the stove. "I'll carry my shoes. I don't mind carrying my shoes. Who cares if I look fancy at seven o'clock in the morning?"

"I care. You look fancy. That's a lovely dress."

"You and I are always carrying our shoes. In case. Just in case." 97
She sounded like Anita. But she laughed naturally. "Are you packed? I thought I heard you packing."

"Yes, sure. I'm wearing my new clothes home."

"That's nice, Ben."

We spoke as if we had never made love, or as if we had made love too long ago to remember. I am sorry, now I am sorry, we did not make love again.

She said, "I called about the planes. I was right. A lot of planes to Columbus. Ten-twenty, two-fifteen, eight-twenty. TWA, through flights. You don't even have to stop in Pittsburgh. It doesn't take any time. A little over an hour, an hour and a quarter. You'll rent a car, won't you?"

"Sure. Sometimes you meet somebody meeting somebody else, going back to Athens." I have always anticipated.

There were jellyfish.

"Careful where you step," Helen said.

They were huge. I have always hated them. I looked at them hard. I stepped carefully. I was trying to tell myself what they were like. They were like death in Jello. Or dead organs under clear plastic.

"But they are beautiful in the water, from a ship," Helen said.

"Yes, I suppose so."

I reached for her hand.

We held hands and walked on the beach.

We talked to each other. I do not remember lying about anything.

"And that's the truth," I said about something.

Helen said, "I know. I'm not being gloomy. We're not being gloomy."

Once Helen said, "We haven't talked about the cottage, my selling the cottage. You were supposed to advise me. But don't. I'll get a little straightened around. I'll make haste slowly."

"That's what my father used to say."

"The nice part about having a lot to say to somebody is that you never finish saying it. And Mr. Kimberly hasn't brought the heaters."

"That's right."

Nobody mentioned the word *love*. I suppose I should be glad.

We were back in the cottage, having coffee at the kitchen table. I unfolded my paper napkin. It had been folded crookedly.

My father died in a nursing home. The last time I visited him the patients, the inmates, whatever, were having lunch. Each old man and old lady sat in a funeral chair in front of a snack tray. They sat in a room as wide as a beach. They were having meat loaf, and a Jello fruit salad, and two slabs of white bread, spinach, and coffee. The dishes and silver were plastic. I had never visited the nursing home at mealtime before.

I stood beside my father although I had been offered a chair. He said, "I wish you'd sit down, Ben."

"I'm great. I can talk to you better this way." The others in the room were eating quietly. I shouted. "You're doing great. You'll be out of here in no time, and back at the office. Just you wait and see."

My father touched his plastic knife and fork and spoon. He straightened them until they lay neat as a picture for silver in a television commercial. He said, "I wish you wouldn't talk so loud, boy."

He unfolded his napkin and folded it again and placed it on the left side of his plate, smoothing it.

The nurse, waitress, whatever she was, a tall woman with a mustache, came to my father's chair. "Isn't everything delicious, Dad? What's the matter? Everybody else is eating good. And we're going to have jelly roll for dessert." She winked at me. She jarred my father's snack tray. The gray coffee splashed from his plastic cup.

My father did not swear. He unfolded his napkin and began to daub at the tray, spilling more coffee.

"Here, wait," the woman said. "We mustn't be clumsy. Here's another napkin, sweetheart." She winked again as if we had a secret.

I said, "Well, it's good to see you, Dad. I'm glad you're getting along so well. I wish I didn't have to rush."

I said to Helen, "We haven't mentioned me last night. I'm . . . I'd rather mention it. I don't know . . . ." She was not helping me. "The crying."

"Funny Ben. Nobody remembers it. Here, let me warm up your coffee. And then we'd better set out. If we're going to make the ten-twenty."

"It's been a nice visit." I was Anita.

"Hasn't it, though?"

We kept having a nice visit, clear to Philadelphia. It was a visit, that's what it was, the way people used to visit people, Mrs. Hathaway and Mrs. Phalp. We were both pleased, for instance, with the Turtle Crossing signs. We could have been Mrs. Phalp and Mrs. Hathaway.

Helen let me out in front of the terminal. I do not approve of long leave-takings. I hate the way Anita leaves a party. It is like tearing off bandages slowly.

Helen said, "I'd love to come in with you. I know that's silly. I'd be glad to drive you on to Athens. I know that's sillier. I hope your plane's on time."

"It will be." I had taken my suitcase from the back seat. I was on the sidewalk. "I guess this is all. I keep feeling I had more luggage."

"I know. It's that way. I'm always feeling I'm leaving packages."

She had not turned off the engine. "Give my love to Anita."

"I will. And you'll come back to see us."

"And the girls. Love to the girls."

"Yes, of course."

She did not seem to be in a hurry, but she must have pressed her foot against the accelerator. A plane flew over us. Perhaps it was the plane's engine. She had moved her purse and gloves to the place I had been sitting.

I reached into the car. She leaned over. I watched my arm in its orange sleeve. We shook hands. I looked at her face. She was smiling. We were both smiling.

I am a very goddamned romantic son of a bitch. I am Mr. America. I want everything, all ways. I am also a good man. I am the meek. I inherit the earth.

I can remember when you could look up words in the dictionary and find meanings for words, like *good* and *depraved*.

I am also, perhaps, still a little hungover.

We have a very old dictionary here at the cabin.

I went into the terminal. In a dressing room, for a coin in a slot, I changed into my light-blue shirt, the maroon necktie, my dark jacket. In exchange for other monies a porter gave me a half-pint of Jim Beam. I waited in the stall until he brought me the bottle. I drank half of the bottle.

I went, sedate, into the waiting room to allow a microphone's voice to announce flight number One Four Three.

I drank again, in a stall, to the two-fifteen, flight number Five Four Seven.

A man could do worse than sit for a day in an airport. I did not eat or sleep.

Sitting for a day in an airport is not unlike writing a story.

I am blessed. I have been blessed.

The eight-twenty, flight number Five Seven Three, was a good flight. I sat by myself. Perhaps I muttered to myself, sitting by myself. The hostess was named Betty Kortlander. I asked her name.

At Columbus I was at the National Car Rental desk, the only rental desk that has heard of Athens, Ohio, when Dorothy Cooper said, "What on earth are you doing here, Ben Adams?"

I sobered. I was back home. I am sober at home.

She had met her brother from Maine. Red, the brother, was waiting for his luggage. Dorothy said, "Of course you'll ride with us."

I sat in the back seat of Dorothy's Thunderbird. It was a very uncomfortable automobile. Dorothy is a pal of Anita's, a telephone pal. She has a long and sharp tongue. I rather like her. Red was affable. Red swears easily. I listened to them. I made appropriate remarks. Dorothy considers me, I gather, something of a wag. Dorothy said we must get together soon. I explained carefully about Anita's being away. Dorothy said she was sorry. Dorothy said she didn't know what was happening to June, it was almost over, and she was clear back in May. Dorothy and I are wags. Perhaps we could have met often. I do not like Dorothy.

Dorothy insisted on driving me clear out home.

I leaned forward. I imagined Helen's car in the driveway.

Dorothy said, "I think you have company."

I thought, "My heart stopped," as books used to say.

There was only the Volks in the driveway.

We are electrified. Even when we are at home a light goes on in the living room at nine; two lights appear in the house downstairs at ten. We seem at home to callers, even to strangers or death, even when we are away. At one the house goes dark. We are full of lights. We want everyone to imagine we are at home.

"You'll come in for a drink."

They came into the lighted house for a drink. The house was immaculate. "Imagine leaving in a rush and having a house look like this!" Dorothy kept saying. "Graham would give his heart and soul if I could have a house look like this. Well, another one, just a small drink, just a smidgen."

"I don't care if I do," Red said, "but easy on the soda. Soda's bad for a man's stomach."

I did not want them to leave.

It was one o'clock. The lights blinked off in the house downstairs while I stood on the patio. I was frightened. I thought somebody human had turned off the lights. I thought Helen waited on the stairway.

It was too late to call Anita. I didn't know where to call Anita.

I imagined Anita and Ernie. I tried to imagine them together.

I took off my traveling clothes and put on my swimming trunks and my new brown shirt and my orange sweater. I unpacked my traveling case.

I walked both houses, the upstairs house and the downstairs house. I stopped and looked at window facings and mantels and furniture. I studied Anita's bathroom, the cosmetics and medicines on her shelves. I studied my bathroom. I studied the girls' bathroom. I said foolish sentences like, "Who would not consider himself blessed? Who would consider himself blessed?"

I could not remember having been in the house alone.

Despite the fact that Anita and I have agitated together over most of the furnishings, I did not recognize many of them. The house is over ten years old. Perhaps I am not. I said that kind of sentence aloud.

I reached back to turn off lights behind me, assuring myself first that lights burned in front of me.

Ernie helped with the electrical arrangements. Ernie is a mechanical man.

I said, "Only men who are blessed can allow themselves the luxury of guilt." I was repeating myself. I felt no guilt except the guilt of being blessed.

Some of the sentences I said are no doubt true.

I slept for a long time, in my clothes, on our king-sized bed, which allows us to sleep both separately and together.

Anita had, of course, taken her address book with her. The far left cubbyhole of the lower shelf of the mahogany desk, which had belonged to her great-grandmother, was empty.

"Somebody named Ransom," I could say to the operator. "A funeral home. A crematorium? The airport, where you rent helicopters."

I dialed Information.

"Information," she said crossly. "What city?"

I lowered the receiver gently. I looked over my shoulder, hoping to be sure I had lowered the receiver without bothering anybody.

I packed my traveling case.

I drove to this cabin. I assumed it was midmorning, but I was not sure. I am not sure. I deliberately left my wristwatch on the bedside table.

It was afternoon for a long time. It was night for a long time, and Anita called. It has been day for a long time. It has stopped being day.

I have no idea how long it takes for a man who types easily to write a log, or a journal, or a story.

The man is impossibly tired.

The man has a toothache.

The man looks young. Many people have said, Ernie has said, "You can't be that old."

Men tell on women to pretend that men are young.

103

Anita and Ernie do not sleep together. Jealousy is a greater luxury than guilt.

I do not believe in narratives that pretend to be confessions. I do not believe, "I write these words to find out who I am; I write to explain or discover."

Everybody knows himself, at least his monogram. I do not believe many stories. I read for the final pleasure of disbelief, disapproving.

I have tried to write these words cold.

If Anita should read these pages, if Helen should read these pages, Ernie, the girls—my God.

And yet I have enjoyed what I have done.

And I believe that any man who writes hopes for a reader.

A man who writes a diary, even in code, imagines a reader, daring. I do not believe a man raises dogs or fashions a banjo clock only for his own amusement. He expects objects to be attended.

I suppose here, in the dark, I am believing in the community of poor fellows. I have no right to call myself pathetic. I have chosen.

Perhaps I am writing a story. Perhaps I am making it up, hoping somebody will believe it.

I have finished a manuscript, I am finishing. I keep writing, hoping the book will not end, like a birthday when you are twelve or an affair when you are almost forty-five.

I could tear the manuscript into little pieces. I could hire a plane to scatter the ashes over Lake Burr Oak.

I could buy a paper shredder. These days frugal old Ben Adams could buy almost anything he took a mind to.

I could put the manuscript into a brown manila envelope. I could address it to somebody, the stewardess on the airplane who gave me two drinks and a pillow.

104   Her name was Betty Kortlander.

I am remembering the science fiction novels.

I could walk into a lake. I could disappear, sitting on the front deck, into the trees. I can imagine nobody's looking for me.

I would like to imagine a stranger on Court Street, or one of the people in the Philadelphia airport, reading what I have written. I have not mentioned any of the people in the airport. I am close to those people who waited through the day.

I would like for somebody to say, "Ben Adams."

I like the idea of a typewriter.

I type easily.

I love Anita Vimont Adams.

Ben Adams and Helen Cunningham left Athens, Ohio, on Friday morning. They had an affair. Ben returned to Athens on Monday night. His wife was away. She was in Lexington, Kentucky, with his friend and employee, Ernie Hill, his children, Tina and Margot. In a little while, in a few minutes, Ben should probably try to make telephone calls to people. He is tired now.

He is tired enough to drive into Athens, Ohio, and mail a manuscript and, later, walk into a lake.

Ben Adams is a Victorian. Not many people understand Victorians. But they exist.

The Girls

Today is Friday, December 14, 1979.

I write at my wife's behest.

I have always said I wanted time to write. Anna has reminded me of my desire to write, at least twice a day for the past twenty-one days.

Anna and I are displaced persons, aliens. We belong, as much as we are capable of belonging, in Graham, Kentucky. We are living in Houston, Texas.

When I was a child I assumed I would not have to die until I was thirty-three, Jesus' age, incidentally the age of our son Archer now. I remember saying to myself on my eleventh birthday, "You have twenty-two more years."
    I could not imagine anyone's being sixty years old.
    I still find the age difficult to imagine.

Our first son is named Archer Lee Baxter, our only living son. His brother, Mark Lytelle Baxter, was killed on his bicycle, November 7, 1961. We are also the parents of Charlotte Thomas Baxter, who is in her early twenties, a graduate student at Ohio University.

I write at a built-in vanity dresser, in a one-room apartment, Sky-view No. 7. At home we rarely lock our doors. In Houston, Texas, whose name should be Sin City according to Aunt Gloria, we lock our doors.

Our son Archer, who lives in Manhattan, has published three nov-els. Last night he called from Beverly Hills, where he serves as a kind of adviser for the filming of his first novel, *Eleven*. Archer takes neither himself nor the project very seriously. He is coming to Houston on December 23. Mother, Aunt Gloria, Anna, and I are delighted.

Anna says it will be nice for me to have a man around, although I have not complained about my life among the ladies.

There is a slight chance that my sister, Phoebe, four years youn-ger than I, will attend us. Phoebe is a sometimes actress, living in Boston.

The students at Graham College, in Kentucky, are preparing to leave for their Christmas holiday. Were I at home, Ray Fletcher and I would be having a little flurry of business at The Bookstore, sell-ing Christmas items from the Reduced table, a few books. Ray is this minute, I assume, checking lists, worrying over whether the textbooks for the second semester will arrive in time.

The Bookstore is in good, if agitated, hands. Ray is an efficient young bore who will grow to be an efficient old bore.

I have been connected with The Bookstore most of my adult life. I now own it. It is a pleasant store. I am surprised at how little I have thought about the store these past three weeks.

Anna has kept saying she would be satisfied if I wrote "just any-thing," little essays, a longish *Dailyaide*. "Copy something—just so long as it's writing."

For the past twenty-five years we have kept a diary of sorts in a book named *Dailyaide,* from Woolworth's. The records of our lives together rest on the top shelf of the bookcase in the spare room at home. I cannot remember ever having taken down one of the vol-umes. Anna dusts them twice a year, spring and fall.

The *Dailyaides* are well put together, a page for each day of the year, accompanied by an unmemorable quote.

"'The best is good enough.'—German."

"'He is well paid that is well satisfied.'—Shakespeare."

"Make every day a cheerful day."

There is no source for the "every day" quotation. I assume everybody or nobody said, "Make every day a cheerful day."

There are twenty-seven lines for saying what it means to be alive all of one day.

Most of the pages of our *Dailyaides* are empty. The books start well. Our Januarys are often rather fully recorded; then come the white pages, followed by a scattering of notes in May, a few more for October; December includes the Christmas presents we have received, the people we have had to dinner.

It will soon be time to buy a new *Dailyaide* for ourselves and The Girls, to wrap the books in paper left over from other Christmases—Anna has brought old Christmas paper with us—to write on cards, "Guess What?" "Surprise!"

Anna says she will keep up the 1980 *Dailyaide* if I write "something."

I am writing.

My name is Arch, or Archie, Lee Baxter. Nobody calls me Archer. Archer is my son.

The Girls' accident—we came to think of it as The Accident—happened two Mondays before Thanksgiving, November 12.

Through the years we have talked to Mother and Aunt Gloria every week or ten days. Generally we have called them on the weekends when the rates were lower. We have written every week: Anna, on Wednesday; I, on Sunday afternoons. Mother has written us every Monday. "A proper family communicates," Mother has said and said.

I have felt that the telephoning was an unnecessary luxury. Better, I have thought, to add thirty or forty dollars a month to the quarterly checks we send them: we call the checks Valentines, Birthday gifts, Labor Day and Christmas presents, to save everybody's feelings. The Girls are fond of long distance conversations, even though we merely repeat what we have already written. Anna insists that the calls mean a great deal to The Girls. And so we have kept calling.

For years The Girls have visited us in June and December. They have stayed for varying lengths of time, from two weeks to two months. We have planned the years around them. Never have they told us how long they were going to stay.

I have said to Anna, "They'll leave when they're bored with us. You're too good to them."

"I'd be ashamed, Arch. Your own mother, and your own Aunt Gloria. They're no trouble."

Mother and Aunt Gloria are gracious, charming, good company, and trouble.

Through the weeks of their visits Anna's face tightens, her back hurts increasingly. And she has kept planning still another divertissement—a day at Shakertown or My Old Kentucky Home, a dinner party for ladies. Men, somebody's father or uncle, used to be included in the festivities. Now there are only the old ladies left, bearing in their purses pictures of grandchildren and great-grandchildren.

"We certainly don't require all this entertainment," The Girls have said. But they have expected it.

We had not seen The Girls for a year. Mother didn't feel quite up to the June trip. "Nothing serious. I'm perfectly well. But we'll be there Christmas. Keep a light in your window."

We worried over her, but not lengthily. We went to Canada for two weeks.

On Sunday night, November 11, The Girls sounded in fine fettle.

The next weekend the Hobarts from Louisville visited us. Lurene

Hobart is Anna's chief relative, although she is only a first cousin once removed. The Hobarts are warming people. We had company for dinner on both Saturday and Sunday nights.

Mother's Monday letter was brief but jolly. It was Indian summer again in Houston. Could we imagine that? She said we shouldn't bother to call on the weekend, why not wait until Thanksgiving? Charlotte would be there, wouldn't she? How on earth was her granddaughter Charlotte, the naughty child who never wrote? "We can all talk, kill several birds with one stone, as it were. I worry about your telephone bill."

Charlotte had called several weeks earlier to proclaim that she was coming, bringing a fellow graduate student. He was named Timmy. Timmy was a sculptor. He did absolutely marvelous things with Styrofoam and soda straws and ceramics and plaster.

Long ago we learned not to believe in Charlotte's proclamations.

She and Timmy decided a week before Thanksgiving that they should fly to San Diego. Timmy needed to visit the zoo. Timothy was suddenly into animals. Charlotte was breathless. "If I could have my December and January allowances, it would certainly be appreciated."

Charlotte is twenty-two years old.

When I was twenty-two . . . but never mind.

On the upstairs extension Anna sighed.

I said, "Okay. But we'll miss you."

Anna said coldly, "Have a good trip."

Anna keeps maintaining that Charlotte is a grown woman. Often Anna says, "I've washed my hands of that child Charlotte." Again and again Anna reminds herself that she has washed her hands of Charlotte.

Charlotte said, "I'll see you Christmas. I can't wait for Christmas. Keep a light in your window."

Poor Charlotte.

We did not know about The Accident until Thanksgiving.

Archer called from California at eight in the morning. He had not been to bed yet. He said he wanted to be the first to wish us happy Thanksgiving. He was having a good time. They were about to

finish with the jiggly picture show: "Don't expect anything much."
Archer sounded as usual, relaxed, friendly. Anna always says,
"Archer is the sweetest and easiest person in the world."

Anna yelled at me from upstairs that we should talk to The Girls
while we were at it.

Mother answered. "And a happy Thanksgiving to you, Archie
Lee. Guess where I'm talking from?"

On the extension Anna said, "I can't imagine, Mil. The
chimney? The front porch?"

"Guess again, Dilly."

For no logical reason I am annoyed by the Mil and Dil names.
Anna defends Mother. Over and over she explains that she didn't
know what to call her mother-in-law. Mother made up the names on
our wedding day. Anna considers them clever, cute. Mother-in-law
and Daughter-in-law. Mother and Anna are fine together.

I said, "Quit teasing, Mother. Where?"

"My bed. My very own bed. I'm home from the hospital."

Anna and I said, "Hospital?" at the same time.

"Needles, pins." Mother was chortling. "The fool doctor said I
was getting along so well I could come home tomorrow, and I said I
was ready to come home that minute. And he let me."

Aunt Gloria was on her telephone. "Trixie Billis almost killed
us. She tried to kill us. Donna Dale wouldn't let me call you."

"Hush, Gloria. I was in the hospital for ten days, and I'm just
fine, and you aren't to give it another thought. The hospital was
utterly pleasant; marvelous food."

Anna said, "We'll come right away."

Mother said, "You'll do nothing of the kind. You've never been
less needed anywhere. We're perfectly fine. Let me tell you about
it."

We talked for over an hour. The Girls were not to be hurried in
their duet recital.

Anna and I knew about Trixie Billis. Trixie was Presbyterian,
too. Mother had met her at the LLL, Live Long and Like It Club, a
group that gathered at the church for tea and sandwiches every
Thursday afternoon. Trixie had become Mother's chauffeur.

Mother had written that some of the old fools danced and played table tennis, "but all in all a pleasant group. Your Auntie Gloria won't attend. Gloria is working at being a heathen."

Trixie drove a pale-blue Cadillac. Huge. She was not a very good driver, although everything was automatic.

Mother and Aunt Gloria were Trixie's projects, her good deeds. Trixie drove them to the laundromat, over on Kentucky Avenue, every Monday morning.

"It's not far. Trixie has to do her own washing anyhow, although she has a maid. Colored. We aren't a burden. Sometimes she gets on our nerves. Gloria's particularly. She's always bringing us goodies."

Trixie had not stopped at a stoplight. She had driven herself and Mother and Aunt Gloria squarely into a camper whose sides were painted with three hills and two moose and a waterfall.

"There were two waterfalls, Donna Dale."

"All right, one or two. It was all Trixie's fault, absolutely. Such a nice young man was driving. He had a nice young girl with him. They were on their way to Galveston. They came to see me in the hospital. They're just good friends, but I think they're going to get married."

Trixie had walked away from the accident, straight away. She was wearing those high heels, platform, the red ones. An ambulance had taken Aunt Gloria and Mother to the Methodist hospital; they rode together in the ambulance. Aunt Gloria had never been so shaken in her life. Trixie had hailed a cab. "There she was, waiting for us at the hospital, not a hair out of place. And my poor little sister with a broken pelvis."

"Gloria, tell the truth. They were afraid my pelvis was injured somewhat."

"Broken. You mean broken, Donna Dale. They were afraid they would have to operate."

"Injured. Merely injured. I'm just a little stowed up."

Aunt Gloria said, "They dismissed me right away. A little pip-squeak of a doctor told me to take an aspirin and a nap."

I said, "We can be there in no time. I think we ought—"

"Listen to me, Archie Lee. This is your mother speaking. You aren't to set foot in this direction. We'll let you know if we need you. I promise. It's been a kind of outing."

I asked Aunt Gloria if Mother were telling the truth.

Mother said, "Of course I'm telling the truth. Now let me talk to that Miss Charlotte."

Mother, ebullient over her hospital outing, accepted the news that Charlotte was in San Diego at the zoo. I quoted Charlotte exactly, except for the allowance request. I figured that Mother would find out about Timmy at Christmas.

I have not washed my hands of Charlotte, but I've grown weary of reinterpreting her activities for friends and loved ones.

Being a parent to Charlotte Thomas Baxter has not been simple.

Mother said, "How good for her to get some sunshine. She can visit with Archer while the young man works with his animals."

Mother's innocence is surely total.

I am sure that Mother assumed that my sister, Phoebe, went virginal to her several marriage beds. Mother assumes that all people go virginal to their marriage beds.

Aunt Gloria was saying that the ladies next door were bringing turkey dinner.

Mother said, "And that's another pleasant thing to think about. We are very blessed. And whom are you having for dinner?"

Anna took over. Anna does not mind talking on the telephone.

Mother was delighted that we were having the minister and his wife, two foreign students, and Ray Fletcher. What were we having to eat? Anna told her. How was our weather? Anna told her.

I said, hoping to end the conversation, "We'll keep in touch, every day."

"Arch! Twice a week is quite sufficient. You hear me. You can hear me, Arch?"

"You'll be here for Christmas, of course."

"Of course." Mother was giggling. "There's life in the old girl yet."

Anna said, "Silly Milly."

Mother said, "It's been a year since I've laid eyes on you. I've never been away from my bairnies so long before." She coughed.

Considering exigencies, I said, "We don't know what Archer and Charlotte are up to yet. For Christmas."

"Naturally, you don't," Mother said. "They are very busy young people."

I suppose Anna and I had each decided that we would have to go to Houston before we hung up the receivers.

Thanksgiving dinner was a disaster. The minister and his wife were dieting; the Pakistani student was a vegetarian; the Japanese boy, who laughed a great deal, seemed to know only one word: *frexible;* and Ray Fletcher, never the life of any party, good man though he be, spent the afternoon sneezing: "I'm allergic to something in this room, or someone," he kept saying.

Fortunately, the company left early.

While we overloaded the dishwasher, cleaned up the kitchen, we kept telling each other that there was no need to worry about Mother.

Anna said we really should have taken up the Hobarts on the trip to Florida. We were old enough to give ourselves a nice long vacation somewhere warm.

I agreed.

Anna said that Ray could certainly manage The Bookstore by himself.

There was no arguing about that. Ray's attention to details is as total as Mother's innocence.

Anna said we could stay away a month, two months.

I said, "Surely not that long."

Anna said, "The store is going terribly well, isn't it, Arch? Even if you don't like to admit it."

I said, "You haven't heard me complaining."

"And Charlotte and Archer, if they deign to bless us with their presence—they could come down at Christmas. Can you imagine going swimming on Christmas Day?"

I said, "You don't go swimming in Houston. It gets as cold there as it does here."

"We're talking about Florida." Anna studied the dishwasher controls as if she had never seen a machine of its kind before.

I said, "The idea is absolutely preposterous, damn it."

"Arch, I didn't say—"

"Two people, sixty years old, giving up the house and business they've worked their tails off for . . . to be baby-sitters. Sixty-year-old baby-sitters."

117

"I'm just newly sixty. And I wasn't saying—"

"Of course you were. Of course you are. They'll eat us up. We're not that strong. We owe ourselves." I wasn't looking at Anna. And then I looked at her.

"Oh, Anna." We put our arms around each other.

Anna said, "I was just saying . . . if worse comes to worst . . ."

"I know."

Something broke in the dishwasher.

Anna said, "It's probably just a jelly glass."

We laughed together.

Anna was right. It was just a jelly glass.

We talked to Mother and Aunt Gloria every other evening.

The Monday after Thanksgiving, Mother said she was up and around and feeling bouncy, thank you. She had had a little flare-up with that silly hiatal hernia—she had overeaten; the little flare-up was the result of nothing but gluttony. Trixie had brought mince pies, darling little pies not much bigger than a silver dollar. A person ate five of them before she realized what she was doing. Mother talked at length about the pies.

Aunt Gloria was so quiet that Anna asked, "Are you still there, Aunt Gloria?"

"I'm letting Donna Dale do the talking. Donna Dale is the authority around here."

Mother said, "Silly Gloria. She clucks over me like a mother hen," and turned to a discussion of the weather.

I told myself not to make anything of Aunt Gloria's quietness. Her sulking could have been the result of a quarrel over how long a pot roast should be cooked.

Friday night, November 30, we were ready for bed when Aunt Gloria called. Her voice can sound more wan than any voice Charles Dickens ever imagined. She was whispering. "I just want you to prepare yourselves. We've had the doctor—I've had the doctor, the real doctor, not the pipsqueak. He left about an hour ago. Donna's asleep now. Dr. Swardson *said* it was probably the hiatal hernia. But it was a heart attack."

I said, "I can catch a plane." It was difficult to control my voice,

118

even though I kept telling myself that Aunt Gloria delights in exaggerating illnesses.

Anna had gone downstairs. She was saying, "We'll come. There's a Delta from Lexington at eight tomorrow."

I said, "We'll be there."

For years, on the underside of my mind, I have waited for the announcement of my mother's death.

I love my mother, although I do not pretend to know what love means. I have depended on her and she has depended on me, surely a part of the definition of love. I was twelve years old when my father died. Mother and Phoebe and I lived in various houses together for all of my youth and young manhood. I attended Graham College, living in our houses. I came home from the war to Mother. When Anna and I married, Anna moved into a house with Mother and me. For two years we three lived together in more harmony than I had dared imagine, infinitely more than I can imagine now.

It would be pleasant to give myself credit for the frequent happinesses of those two years, and of the summer and winter visits that have juggled three generations of us. But the credit is all Anna's and Mother's.

Anna became a daughter to Mother, Mother became her actual mother. For me, Mother has continued to be a kind of other wife.

At the downstairs telephone Anna said, "We'll be there. The flight number is—"

Aunt Gloria regained her normal voice—got hold of her puckering string, as Mother says. "I don't mean today, right now. Donna Dale would kill me if she knew I was calling. I mean, you must prepare yourselves. She's failing." She had so tightened her puckering string that she was able to tell what Mother had said to the doctor. And the doctor had said, "You really know how to sass a fellow." Aunt Gloria was breathing heavily. "I just had to talk to you. Sometimes I get . . . desperate."

I asked her if she had called Phoebe.

"Phoebe?"

"Phoebe. My sister, Phoebe."

"Not yet. I hate to worry her. She has so much on her hands right now. You know about the television business, the contest, the competition."

"We know. We know." I was annoyed.

Several times Phoebe has called us to report the progress of the search for Mrs. Mayonnaise. Her agent was really working on it. If Phoebe won, she would be famous—the residuals would last forever.

Anna said, "Oh, my. I hope she gets it."

I said, "We all do." Anna has taught me, almost taught me, the foolishness of resenting Phoebe's grand projects.

Anna was saying, "You'll be here for Christmas. We're counting the days."

Aunt Gloria's voice collapsed again. "Donna Dale hasn't written you? I thought you knew. We couldn't possibly."

I said, "The idea. Surely."

"We've been hoping maybe . . . maybe you'd come here. It's been a year since you've seen your mother."

I thought, Shit. I said, "We'll see," a sentence Mother has said all of my life, meaning "Probably not" or "No."

How many years have we celebrated the last Christmas? the last birthday? the last look? Yet standing there by Anna's and my bed, I had a sense of The Last Christmas as palpable as if someone held ice to my throat. I was shivering.

I said, "You get in bed and have a good night's rest. We'll see." I said, "We'll do what we can," meaning, "what we feel we must."

"I love you," Aunt Gloria said. "I love you and Dilly."

"We love you," Anna said. "Sweet dreams."

Anna did not come upstairs immediately. I started to call to her. Not risking the sound of my voice, I put on a robe and slippers and stumbled downstairs. Anna had not turned on any lights. I reached for the hall switch, decided against the light. Anna relishes the dark. Often she rids up the kitchen with no light at all.

Perhaps I am afraid of the dark.

"Anna. Anna?"

Five times I called her.

"I'm here in the kitchen, Arch. I'm coming up."

I did not ask her what in the world she was doing in the dark.

It took a moment for my eyes to find her. She leaned her forehead against the telephone on the wall.

"I'm looking at a painting named *Darker on Dark*," I thought, trying to skip the experience of the moment.

I said, "It'll work out."

"We're going, aren't we? To Houston? We must, mustn't we?"

I said, "We'll see," and then I said, "I guess so. I hate like hell . . ."

"It's necessary. We'll have a nice time. Poor things."

I said, "Maybe. Maybe we're damn fools. What if they didn't have us? They'd get along."

"But they do have us."

The *Darker* moved toward me from the merely *Dark*.

Sometimes I can feel Anna's tears in my own throat. "Are you crying?"

"Of course not. I just cry over silly things, you know that. It's just . . ."

"We don't have to be damn fools. A person owes the past only so much. There are hospitals in Houston. Nursing homes. We don't have to be damn fools. We're old too, Anna."

"It's just . . ." I was glad I could not see Anna's face. "Sometimes you feel a big hunk of something is . . . over. You can hear it click out, almost. I just . . . feel bad that a hunk is . . . over. I mean, could be over. It's all happened so fast, Arch."

Anna's hands were the ice at my throat. She said, "I love you." Her lips were as cold as her hands.

I said, "You're cold as ice. You'll catch pneumonia. You won't be any good to anybody if you catch pneumonia."

"You're a funny old thing, Arch. I'm all right. I'm a funny old thing too. But I'm fine, I'm just fine. It will be like a vacation. We've been in a rut, Arch. I'm absolutely just fine. I promise you."

"Come off it, Anna. It'll be terrible."

"It won't, Arch. I was just being sad for The Girls. Maybe for us, too."

We were a long time going to sleep.

The Girls were ecstatic over our decision. "An answer to prayer," Aunt Gloria roared. Mother said, "What joy. What an absolute joy." Aunt Gloria said, "When are you coming? Can we look for you tomorrow?"

I reported the details Anna and I had worked out during the long night. "We couldn't possibly get away until Monday. No, we aren't going to fly. We figure we'll need a car."

"Goodie, goodie." Aunt Gloria reverted to the baby talk I considered funny when I was very young. "Doody, doody, dum-dwop. How heavenly it will be to have a car again."

Mother's voice was suddenly mournful. "I'm just sick at heart we don't have a proper bedroom for you. Gloria's been investigating rentals. We can get a foldaway cot; one of you can sleep on the couch. There'll be plenty of room."

We had anticipated almost everything they were saying.

"No, Mil," Anna said.

Through the night I had told Anna that we must be firm with The Girls, that we must protect ourselves.

"No, Mother. We'll stay at a motel the first night, Wednesday, and then we'll rent a little apartment, someplace close by."

"I'll not hear of it! The idea of your own flesh and blood staying in a motel. The idea, Archie Lee!"

"We won't have it any other way," Anna said. I was proud of her. "You need your rest. You don't need a houseful of company traipsing around."

"The children know what's best for them, Donna Dale. We'd adore to have you here, but you know where you'll be most comfortable." Aunt Gloria was taking charge. "There's a motel a couple of blocks away. I'll make a reservation. Wait a sec. I'll get a pencil and write the date down."

Mother said she felt better already. She felt like dancing a jig.

Anna said, "Arch will be doing some writing," although I had asked her not to mention her notion of my writing. "He'll need to spread out."

"How very nice," Mother said.

Aunt Gloria had found her pencil. "Wednesday. Oh, joy." And then she asked the question we knew she would ask, the question we have been too delicate to ask her through the years of her visiting us:

122   "How long are you going to stay?"

Anna said, "Through Christmas."

"Doody, doody. We'll get you down here and we'll just keep you."

Mother said, "What else? What else should we know?"

Aunt Gloria inquired about our weather. She reported that their weather had been absolutely lovely.

I asked if it would be warm enough to go swimming on Christmas day, to Aunt Gloria's further merriment.

"And what about Archer and Charlotte?"

"We don't know. We'll keep in touch."

"Those rascals." Aunt Gloria was convulsed. Everything was funny to Aunt Gloria that night.

Leaving home for three weeks, or six, or two months was not funny. "What if it's three months?" I asked Anna. She said I was a Gloomy Gus.

I had no trouble with Ray Fletcher and the store. The college was to close for vacation on December 14. The students would not be back for a month. Ray's round little eyes glistened when I proposed his taking full charge for a while. Ray, as indelicate as Aunt Gloria, asked, "How long is *for a while?*"

I said, "We'll see. We'll hire a couple more students, part-time. You don't mind, do you?"

Ray didn't mind at all.

But leaving a house for an undetermined time is more difficult than leaving a store.

We are the satisfied owners of two oldish cars, a '73 Valiant, four doors, and a '76 Volkswagen. At first we said that we would take the Volkswagen, what with the price of gasoline, what with the possibility of no gas at all. We would pack a big and a little suitcase apiece, and that would be that.

But Anna decided that we ought to take household things if we were going to keep house: a few pots and pans, blankets, lamps—rented places were always short on lamps—books, indeed books; and, oh yes, typewriter paper; and some summer clothes—maybe we would get to Florida, if everything worked out.

Neither of us defined what "worked out" could mean.

Neither of us said, "If The Girls should die . . ." We acted as if The Girls would discover health in three, six weeks—two months at the very most, as if the world would last forever.

123

We decided to take the Valiant. It would be ever so much more comfortable for The Girls if they wanted to take little rides.

Anna kept her promise of the dark kitchen night. She was just fine. I told her she was so fine she was driving me crazy. She canceled and arranged for dental appointments, club meetings, Christmas commitments such as the decoration of the church, the mail, the newspaper, the garbage collection. She took the old Olivetti to The Typewritery for overhauling: she bought two extra ribbons.

"You can write all day, Arch. Archer is a writer because you have inspired him. Those book reviews you wrote for the *Courier*. Archer was proud of you."

"Come off it, Anna."

"It's a way of saving time. You can *save* time, Arch, for both of us. That's what writing is."

"Damn it, Anna."

"And every night I'll read what you've written. Just anything. It's a working vacation. And then Florida, maybe."

I spent most of Sunday afternoon wedging objects into the trunk and the back seat of the car.

Anna insisted that the typewriter ride between us. She didn't want it to get jostled out of kilter, she said.

All afternoon I alternated between the giddiness of the prospect of travel and a deep depression over its foolishness.

Anna is right. I do not transport well.

But the trip to Houston was as blessedly uneventful as a trip can be.

We took turns driving. Anna is a good driver, better than I, she maintains. But she takes a cavalier attitude toward speed limits; and she notices in detail more objects—such as birds and landscapes—than necessary. She can spot a meadowlark a quarter of a mile away, on the far right.

We stop often for rest rooms and coffee.

The first day we drove four hundred seven miles, no distance for Ray Fletcher, but good for us. We were accepted at the first motel. I always worry over finding a place, positive that the town is having a Shrine convention and the state fair.

"Posh and dumb-dumb," Anna said. "They don't have state fairs in December. Everybody's at home getting ready for Christmas."

The motel was expensive but clean.

The second day we managed four hundred twenty miles. The motel was expensive and dirty. Neither of us slept much. "We're just journey-proud," Anna kept saying. "Think of something pleasant and count your breaths."

I imagined a lazy river in midsummer, and almost immediately someone was drowning in it. I counted to three thousand.

We slept until seven. Snow spit against the vast window. I said, "That isn't real snow," and I said, "Look at that filthy snow."

After five minutes of my mouthing Anna said that we should get up and hit the road.

"In all that snow?"

Anna said, "Very small snow. It's not sticking. There'll be little traffic. The roads won't be slippery."

Always Anna speaks with authority about traffic patterns and road conditions, even in foreign countries. Always I am annoyed with her, even though, or particularly though, she is often right.

We boiled hot water with our Magic Coil, burned our hands as we drank our instant coffee from the motel glasses (I had forgotten to pack our mugs); we ate an orange apiece, using rough towels as plates and napkins, spilling on ourselves. I have long since ceased mentioning my sense of cheating the management with our in-house breakfasts. Anna is devoted to motel-room breakfasts.

We arrived at the Houston city limits at four o'clock on Wednesday afternoon.

Anna had chattered most of the day. Anna is capable of carrying on lengthy conversations with herself. I know she was trying to make us ignore what we were up to, but I was increasingly less amused or diverted. I said, "You have the map."

"I have the map, a general map, but a map."

"Houston is one city where we do not get lost." I spoke firmly. "It won't be like Indianapolis or Washington, D.C."

"Right. Check, Master."

We got lost several times. Anna is a good guide. I am not always a good follower. She says that when she yells "Right," I turn left seven times out of ten. She exaggerates. But that soggy afternoon I maneuvered a few wrong turns, once reentering by the Do Not Enter lane a thruway I was trying to leave.

Aunt Gloria had made a reservation for us at the Cozy Corners Motel and Restaurant. It was located on Alabama, which was right off Bonita Avenue. Aunt Gloria said we couldn't miss it. I passed Cozy Corners despite Anna's shouting at me, finally found a service station to turn around in, passed Cozy Corners going the other way.

126

Cozy Corners is shaped like an arrowhead, eight rooms in a row, a sharp angle for the office, and eight more rooms. The place shoots itself into the heart of a kind of shopping center. Four of the ten shops bore closed signs in their windows. The lights of the Cozy

Corners' sign were already blinking even though it was two hours before dark. Some of the bulbs had burned out. The sign said Coz Corne.

The manager was cordial, television-Texas cordial. He wore a cowboy hat. His features were bunched together in the center of his wide face; his stomach rolled over his tight blue jeans. He was expecting us. How long were we going to stay? Anna explained that we were looking for a little apartment, but we wanted to be sure he had room for us until we found one. The cordial Texan winked at Anna, "I'll take care of you, little lady, you and your boyfriend."

I tried to imagine a scene in which a weary traveler stamped his fist on the counter and said, "You dumb son of a bitch, you."

I have always thought there is no sense of euphoria like that of the motorist who finally settles into a motel room after a day of driving. Generally Anna and I admire motel rooms extravagantly. Anna has often suggested that we add a motel room to our own house. "I want it to be like every adequate motel room in the world, expectable, no surprises; you know where the bath is, and the drawers and closets are empty, and the bed's made, and the towels are out." Anna delights in her fantasy: the room you don't get ready for company, the room you can move in to when the house gets cluttered.

Anna registered while I brought in our overnight cases. She held the door for me. Mr. Cordiality offered to take us to our room, but I assured him we could find it ourselves. I headed toward the right side of the arrow instead of the left. The Cowboy called to me, "Other way, pardner." Fortunately, Anna did not laugh.

I felt no euphoria at Cozy Corners. Generally we kiss each other as soon as we close a motel door. Generally Anna says, "Lie down. Let me do your back."

We omitted the kiss. I refused the back rub. Anna stood in front of the mirror that reflected the bed. She said, "We ought to unpack. And I look a positive fright. I could rent out as a witch. This hair." Anna was chattering. Her hair is beautiful, white, gleaming, thick. "Did you ever see such a sight?"

I said, "Comb your hair and let's get out of here. We'll walk. Hurry."

I could not wait to see Mother and have it done with.

127

"We ought to call them and say we're here. We don't want to barge in like—"

"They're waiting for us. For God's sake, hurry. It's after four-thirty; it's almost five o'clock."

Aunt Gloria's sense of distance is as vague as her sense of direction. Cozy Corners is not a couple of blocks from Bonita Avenue unless *couple* means eight or ten. True, Bonita is two blocks from Alabama, a main street that contains elegance and squalor, cheek by jowl.

Number 181 Bonita Avenue was left to my Aunt Gloria by her husband, Mr. A. F. Connor, an advance man for the Brown and White Chautauqua, a husband for only one hundred days. Aunt Gloria was living with my parents when Mr. Connor appeared. She was in her twenties, he in his fifties. Mr. Connor died by choking on a fishbone at a Rotary banquet.

Aunt Gloria was not particularly fond of Houston—she kept meaning to leave, but what with one thing and another she never got around to it. She did get around to taking back her maiden name, Archer. "I suppose she prefers to be a maiden lady," Mother said when I quizzed her. "I do not wish to discuss the matter further." Mr. Connor has remained a very dark patch in the history of our family.

It is impossible to believe that Aunt Gloria has lived at 181 Bonita for sixty years, that Mother has lived with her for thirty years.

I have never had patience with people who tell each other that time flies. Of course it does. Dwelling on time's speed has never done anybody any good, except Andrew Marvell, maybe, and a few philosophers.

"Time has flown," I thought as we turned off Alabama, my stomach knotting.

I was not prepared for Bonita Avenue.

Through years of letters and snapshots and vacation conversations, we knew that the street was changing. We knew of the diseased elms, the abandoned warehouse a block away, the nightclub two streets behind 181, the broken sidewalk, the houses that had been turned into rooming places or apartments. Twenty years ago The Girls themselves had converted Mr. Connor's house into two apartments, delighted with themselves, their perspicacity: rental income and no steps to climb.

I assumed that we were up-to-date about Bonita: the student upstairs who was slow about tending to the yard, but quiet; the ladies next door on the right, retired school teachers, lovely ladies, really; the two noisy Mexican families and their brats who lived on the other side; the hippies across the street—"Neither male nor female created He them," Mother had written. "It's a comfortable street withal, run-down at the edges, but comfortable."

I realize that Mother's complaints, like her compliments, have always been qualified. I have not given her credit for that.

Bonita was naked. One blasted elm decorated the first block. Two sodden mattresses lay on the front steps of a corner house. Two mongrels growled at each other over an upturned garbage can.

"Please, Arch," Anna said behind me. "I can't keep up with you."

"Watch that puddle." I turned. Anna's face was as red as if she had been running. Perhaps she had been.

The yard of 181 looked like an abandoned farm lot. I said, "That lazy student."

"I'm sorry. I didn't hear you."

"It doesn't matter."

The concrete floor of the porch was cracked, humped, but the floor shone. Aunt Gloria was at the door.

"Well, look who's here! At last! Bless my soul and body!" She was embracing us. "A sight for sore eyes, if I ever saw such a sight! Donna, they're here. Donna Dale!"

We filled the tiny square of a hall. A dirty stairway rose beside us; its top steps held newspapers and gym clothes and the entrails of a radio.

"Come in. Come right in this minute. Donna!"

The apartment was exquisite: Mother's old furniture, the McGuffey chest, the sugar desk, the rose jar, the pulpit chairs, the shining brass; and there over the couch hung the portrait of Great-great-great-grandmother Essex.

129

I looked down at the new carpet—we had had many telephone conversations about the purchase of the carpet. "The rug is fine." I felt Anna's tears in my throat.

But Anna wasn't crying. "Where's Mil? Where is that good old Mil?"

Mother stood at the door which led off the living room. She held to the doorframe.

She was very thin. I was conscious of her bones. Her flesh seemed to have been draped over her bones. For a moment I thought, "I'm not recognizing her."

"Donna! The walker! Where is your walker?" Aunt Gloria spaced her words, shouting.

"There's the girl," I said.

Aunt Gloria and Anna stepped back. "She shouldn't move without her walker."

Mother was clinging to me, laughing. I was holding soft bones in my arms.

"Archie. My own Archie Lee. The same Archie."

It was every homecoming, from Scout camp, the senior trip to Washington, the army. I could have been ten or seventeen or twenty-four. I could not be a bald man sixty years old.

"And Dilly. Oh, my precious Dilly."

"Mil, Mil, Mil," Anna said, kissing her again and again. Anna was shouting. "What's this about a walker?"

"That fool doctor. I'm totally mended; he couldn't be more pleased with my progress. But he has this idea I'm going to fall."

Both Mother and Aunt Gloria had painted their mouths scarlet; circles of rouge decorated their cheeks.

I said, "You're looking fine. You both are. You're really looking fine."

Mother lifted her hand to her ear. "How's that, Arch?"

"You're looking fine. Just great."

"I'm sorry. I'm not hearing very well. For some words. Just some words."

"You're looking splendid."

"Am I? Am I really? Really and truly?"

"Really and truly. I expected to see an invalid. Here you are cavorting around the house. And the house—it's beautiful." I was shouting.

130

She had been only a little hard of hearing last December.

I thought: She has become a deaf old woman. I could stand the thought by naming it.

I told myself: You can stand a number of thoughts if you keep naming them, slowly, one and two and three.

"How's that, Arch love?"

Aunt Gloria was telling Anna, "She hears less well when she is excited."

"The house is beautiful."

"They must see the house, Gloria. Before we settle down to visit. We think our old things go very well together. Gloria has so many pretty things. And so do I, if I do say so myself. You remember. Grandmother Essex.

"And this is my room. It's marvelously sunny, on sunny days, that is." Her laugh turned into coughing.

The sleigh bed; the coverlet that had belonged to Grandmother Clarke; the gilt-framed mirror; the dressing table with the silver brush, comb, hair receiver, lined up in the exact formation they have held ever since I can remember. On the cherry bedside table was a magnifying glass with a light in it. The room smelled of lilacs.

Mother directed the tour, lurching from doorframe to table to chair to chest. "And here's the little bathroom between our rooms. That tub is the mischief to get out of, but it's very convenient. And Gloria's room with the china closet and more pretty things—no other place to put the china closet."

"Please. Use your walker, Donna."

"Hush, Gloria. You're such an old maid. I'm getting along perfectly, don't you agree, Archie?"

"Fine. Just fine," I said because she was my mother.

"See, Miss Smartie. Archie thinks I'm getting along just fine." She bumped into the Chippendale rocker. I reached toward her, but she righted herself.

"That chair has no business being there. I would like to know what that chair is doing out of place."

In spite of myself, I took her arm. I thought, "She is also an old woman going blind." I could stand that, too. I said, "Here."

"Arch, will you please unhand me? I have been walking for eighty-six years without your aid, thank you very much. And this is

131

the dining room, right off the living room, not much more than a wide space, but quite adequate for the two of us, the four of us." The table was set for four, the blue and white Wedgewood, silver, crystal. A cut glass vase held a single rose in the center of the table.

I said, "It looks like a magazine picture."

"This is Gloria's stuff, the chairs and the table and everything that's on it. The paintings are Gloria's, too. She had a friend who fancied herself an artist. Dead now. Gloria also bought the rose."

"It's all stunning," Anna said behind me. For a moment I had forgot that she was also taking the tour.

"And that's the kitchen." Mother staggered from the table to a rosebacked chair to the doorframe. "This is Gloria's province. It's all very tidy and compact. She won't let me in here any more."

"Something smells divine," Anna said.

"It should. Gloria has been cooking solid for the last three days."

"That is not true, Donna Dale. That is a bald-faced lie."

I was shocked by Anna's laughter. It was not her laughter at all. "You two. You're marvelous."

Mother took my arm. "I didn't mean to be cross, Archie. But I'm so *tired* of being looked after." I suppose she thought she was whispering. "I didn't hurt your feelings, did I?"

I was laughing Anna's laughter, high-pitched and false. We sounded like the clowns on a children's television program. "You couldn't hurt my feelings, you know that." The lie felt good in my mouth.

"Well, I should hope not. You're my Archie Lee."

We had been at the house only a half hour, shouting at each other, when the doorbell rang. A voice called from the hall, "Shave and a haircut, dot dot."

"Oh Lord—Trixie," Aunt Gloria said.

Mother said, "You mustn't talk like that, Gloria."

Aunt Gloria wobbled to the front door.

Aside from Trixie's being the worst driver in the world, we knew that she was over seventy-five if she was a day, and that she dyed her hair magenta and wore a bob suitable for a seventeen-year-old, eighteen at the outside. She was tiny and given to platform shoes with high heels. She was the one who insisted on the dancing at the Live Long and Like It Club. Her husband had been in oil.

"Our family. This is our very own family," Aunt Gloria said.

Trixie, a pretty woman, kissed Mother, Aunt Gloria, and Anna. She stood in front of me. "You look sweet enough to hug and kiss, too." She reached up to hug and kiss me, then rubbed at my cheek. "I didn't mean to get lipstick all over you."

"Tea," Aunt Gloria intoned. "You'll have a cup of tea. It's your tea. You gave it to us last Valentine's Day. We've been saving it."

I was bothered by Aunt Gloria, sure that Trixie would sense she was being ridiculed.

"No, honey. I just brought you a little something for your sweet tooth. I left it on the front porch, on the railing. I was afraid you'd still be having your nappy-byes. I haven't a minute. But I was determined to meet your Archie and his pretty little wife."

I said I would fetch "the little something."

Trixie winked at me. "You're nice. You're nice as The Girls say you are. They're always bragging on you." She rubbed at my face again. "Goodness!"

"The little something" was a vast plate covered with foil heavy enough for insulating an attic. Anna always buys the thinner foil; she says it works just as well.

I stood on the porch for a minute, watching the rain, looking at Trixie's blue Cadillac, which bore no scratches to indicate it had taken Trixie and Mother and Aunt Gloria squarely into a decorated van.

Anna's right. I have a depression mind. I still think coffee should cost a nickel, a loaf of bread a dime.

We have enough income, enough retirement insurance to get along, assuming no disasters. The store does increasingly well. But I stood on the porch wishing I were rich. I was sad that The Girls were having to make do. I cringed over the fact that Anna and I would probably have to search all day for a little apartment that was inexpensive. I was troubled with a pang, like a sudden toothache in the night, that Anna and I had spent our lives, would spend the rest of our lives, with substitutes that "worked just as well." I felt very old.

Aunt Gloria said, "Let me see. Let me have that plate."

The little something was two dozen two-inch squares of Deluxe Miracle Chocolate Supremes on a crystal platter. Aunt Gloria

133

counted the squares. Trixie said they were a recipe she had had "lying around forever." They were really scrumptious—chocolate and crème de menthe and butter. "Mostly butter, Donna Dale. I know how you feel about alcohol, but they don't have any alcohol in them, not really. The cooking burns it out."

Mother did not respond. Trixie paused a moment. In repose, her face stared from her maneuvered body, a skeleton's head.

Anna said, "And marvelously fattening. How I envy you, Mrs. Billis."

"Trixie, Dilly. My name's Trixie." She sparkled again. "I can get into my wedding dress. I'll wear it for you sometime. Size three or four. Can you believe it?"

Aunt Gloria said, "Yes, you've told us. I can believe anything."

"It's from jogging. I jog every day in the world, rain or shine. People recognize me. One old man said he set his clock by me. I shouldn't tell this, but somebody thought I was a teenager. They tried to pick me up."

Anna said, "I'm not surprised." I said, "Of course." Trixie said we were absolutely precious.

Trixie refused to sit down. Mother and Aunt Gloria had settled themselves. Aunt Gloria held the plate in her lap, pinching off little pieces of the Supremes. "I'm not going to offer it around. It will spoil our dinner."

Trixie giggled. "Isn't she a sight?"

For twenty minutes Anna and I stood, telling Trixie good-bye.

We thanked her again for the Supremes. Anna said, "How good of you."

Trixie said, "Donna and Gloria are the ones who are good. Just knowing they're here, their own sweet selves—that's more payment than a person deserves." There were tears in Trixie's mascaraed eyes. She turned to me. "Your folks have the most wonderful sense of humor."

I said, "Thank you."

Nobody mentioned The Accident.

134

"That plate, that little crystal plate," Trixie said when she had finally progressed to the door. "It's a present." She looked at each of us in turn. Obviously she had not intended to leave the plate. "It's a present for . . . Archie. It's a coming-home present."

I stuttered.

"It's Swedish. You look a little Swedish."

Aunt Gloria said, "There's no dealing with her, Arch. Accept it graciously. She wants you to have it. And don't bother with the laundromat Monday, Trixie. They'll take us."

There followed considerable discussion. Trixie finally said, "If you absolutely insist, Gloria."

"I absolutely insist."

Trixie kissed us all good-bye, Mother on the mouth, Aunt Gloria on the ear. Anna and I got kissed on our cheeks.

I followed her to the street, helped her into her huge pale automobile. Trixie said we must keep in touch; it was very important to keep in touch.

In the living room Aunt Gloria said, "She walked away from the accident. She was wearing those high heels, the ones she had on today. And look at your poor mother."

Mother said, "Gloria, we must not lose control of ourselves. You're as bad off as I am. Look at the way you're trembling."

"I am nothing of the sort." Aunt Gloria pushed herself up from her chair. She rearranged the pillows at Mother's back. "Now, if you will all excuse me."

Anna stood. "I'm helping. I can surely do something."

"Sit down, Anna. This is my party. The kitchen's not big enough to whip a cat in. And I have my own ways."

"That's the truth if I ever heard it," Mother said. Aunt Gloria smiled as if she had been complimented.

"But tomorrow, or as soon as we get settled, I'm taking over the kitchen. I'll follow your own ways."

Aunt Gloria looked almost too tired to move, but she leaned over and kissed Anna on the forehead. "You blessed lamb."

I was touched: proud and sorry for, annoyed with, all of us.

Until time for the evening news I bellowed at Mother, Anna spoke naturally. Somehow Anna manages to make Mother hear.

Mother had me turn on the television set. "Louder, just a little louder."

Always, always, Mother used to ask, "What will the neighbors think?"

135

I worried over the quiet student upstairs, even though he was a scoundrel for not tending the yard. I turned the volume higher, worrying about the neighbors up and down the street.

"Better. That's better."

The news, after the manner of the news these weeks, was terrifying.

Mother said, "Surely they'll let those poor hostages out tomorrow."

I said, "Surely."

Aunt Gloria's dinner was a Christmas dinner: turkey, ham, hot rolls, cranberry salad, transparent pie for dessert.

"It's pretty good, Sister. It's really pretty good."

Anna and I complimented every mouthful. I ate two dinners' worth. I was miserable, but pleased that Aunt Gloria was pleased with my appetite.

"You're sure the dressing's all right? Maybe I was a little heavy-handed with the seasoning. Of course you'll have another roll. It's your mother's recipe. Don't you like ham? It's not country ham, but it's ham."

Perspiration matted Aunt Gloria's thin hair. Her hands shook so violently that she had difficulty eating. The tines of her fork clicked against her false teeth. She dribbled tea down her front. But she was pleased. "It is pretty good, if I do say so myself."

Aunt Gloria refused to let us help with the dishes. We insisted too much, perhaps; I felt that Anna was insisting too much. Finally, I said, "When we settle down, I'm going to be the dishwasher. I have no sense of the male role. Or, I consider dishwashing *the* male role."

Mother said, "Archie Lee has always been very good with dishes."

"We'll see, we'll see." Aunt Gloria laughed as if I were a real comedian.

We began to leave at nine-fifteen.

We had a presentation of the keys to the doors, newly made at Woolworth's, downtown Woolworth's, not the one in the shopping center. We were to guard the keys with our lives. Houston, Sin City, was the deepest den of iniquity in the entire United States. Aunt Gloria shivered at the thought of the keys being lost. The blue key opened the porch door, the gold key opened the door into their apartment, the red was for the back door. "Put them on your key ring, Arch. Right now. Let me watch you. Are you sure they're snug?"

I said, "Check and double check," wanting The Girls to laugh, wanting to get out of the steaming apartment.

The Girls were delighted. "Amos and Andy," Mother said. "I don't know when I've thought about them." Aunt Gloria said, "They were wholesome. How I miss them."

I willed Anna not to entertain a discussion of The Negro, Then and Now.

"Ah wah, ah wah, ah wah," Mother drawled, giving one of her best imitations.

Aunt Gloria said, "Those were the days. You can't imagine nigras like Amos and Andy any more."

"They were white men, Gloria."

"I know, I know. But they thought like nigras used to be. The way they used to be, not terrifying a whole city, a whole country."

Anna said only, "About tomorrow . . ."

"Oh yes. What is our schedule for tomorrow? You'll be here for breakfast."

"I'll be here to get breakfast, your way, at eight sharp."

Aunt Gloria clapped her trembling hands. "Doody, doody. In that case we must have a refrigerator and kitchen tour." She pushed herself up from the chair she had just lowered herself into.

Aunt Gloria and Anna were gone a very long time. I roared details of our trip to Mother. She smiled. Her eyes closed, she nodded, jerked herself into waking. "No, I'm not the least bit sleepy. We never go to bed until ten or after. And where did you spend last night?" Mother slept.

In the kitchen Aunt Gloria was telling about The Accident, a story we have now heard in detail at least thirty times. She was saying, "And now poor Donna Dale . . . frail, withered, frail as a reed. There've been times when I thought . . . oh, I don't mean I'm sorry we weren't killed, I don't mean that. But nobody knows . . . oh, blessed Anna."

I stood when Aunt Gloria and Anna came back into the room. "It's time we were going. It's been a long day."

Mother said, "It's the shank of the evening."

I frowned at Anna, daring her to sit down.

"Really, Mil," blessed Anna said. "We're pooped."

Aunt Gloria's eyes were closed. She staggered against me.

I said, "We're going home now, to the motel, I mean. We'll be here at eight. Then we'll start looking for a little place. We won't count on being back for lunch, but we'll have dinner here. Surely we'll find something by then."

"That's the schedule, then. That's settled." Aunt Gloria was bright again. "You have a good head on your shoulders, Archie. Do you understand the schedule, Donna?"

"I am not totally deaf, young lady. Of course I understand."

I was almost too tired to grieve over Mother.

We kissed cheeks. Mother clung to me. "You'll excuse me for not getting up."

Aunt Gloria said, "Until tomorrow. Toodleoo."

We were in the little hallway when Aunt Gloria decided to send some of the pie home with us. "You're likely to get the hungries."

"Really, honestly no," Anna said, but Aunt Gloria was already out in the kitchen.

Mother said, "You have a good voice, Dilly. I'd be the last to speak against my own flesh and blood, but I believe your voice is better than Archie's."

"Good night. Good night."

"Just a sec." Aunt Gloria was rummaging in the drawer of the table by the couch. "They're here somewhere."

Mother said, "Gloria, you're a sight."

"That notepad and pencil. I knew they were here. Write your room number down for us, Archie. We're both a little forgetful."

We left at eighteen minutes after ten.

A streetlight at the corner was out.

The warehouse loomed ominous, twice as vast as it had been in the afternoon.

A car without lights passed us slowly.

I held to Anna's arm.

I was grateful for the drunken lights of Coz Corne.
I cannot remember having been more exhausted.
Anna said, "People don't get tireder than this."
In the motel room we kissed. We kissed as if we were very young people, as if one of us were about to go away somewhere.
We were too tired to bathe, or talk about the evening.

We overslept.

We arrived at 181 at nine o'clock. Cold rain fell. The Girls were waiting for us, each in her own chair, Mother in her lavender robe, Gloria in her yellow.

They were gracious enough, although each of them looked at her wristwatch as we entered. They said they were glad we could sleep. They said sleep was a great blessing.

"Now about that breakfast . . ." Anna was tearing herself out of her raincoat.

"We've eaten," Aunt Gloria said. "Donna Dale is always ravenous at eight A.M."

"Gloria! You're the one who was hungry."

"But we were coming. I promised. I didn't want you to—"

"We don't eat much. Toast and cereal do us just fine. And we're not interested in but two meals a day."

"But the refrigerator is bulging—bacon, eggs . . ."

"We have them on hand for you and Archie Lee. You aren't to give us another thought." Aunt Gloria was disentangling herself from her chair.

Mother, smiling, said, "Come over here and kiss your old Mil and your old Mother. Don't look upset. You don't want to spoil your vacation."

I am surprised at anger. I consider myself mild-tempered. I have considered mildness, when I have bothered to give the matter thought, as no particular virtue: a negative quality, a dislike of the bother of reconciliation, an uninvolvement, a kind of cowardice. I remember the awe I felt for my sister Phoebe's temper fits. When the world didn't go to suit Phoebe, she would clench her fists, squinch her eyes, and scream. Mother would say, in a moderate voice, "Phoebe, dear. Phoebe? Can you hear me, Phoebe?" Obviously Phoebe could not hear. She screamed until she had finished screaming, no longer than a minute or two. On the rare occasions when Mother grabbed her shoulders, shaking her—"Stop that, Phoebe Essex Baxter; you stop that right now!"—Phoebe's screams stopped.

Phoebe held her breath. She could hold her breath for a phenomenal length of time. I can remember saying, "Kiss her or something. Look at what color her face is." I do not remember Phoebe's ever having a temper fit while my father lived.

I was furious with Aunt Gloria and Mother for not having waited for us. In my anger I imagined myself getting The Girls told off. I was amazed at myself. I expelled my breath slowly. I imagined I heard Phoebe's screaming.

Anna kept saying she was mortified; she didn't know when we had pulled such a trick. How could Mil and Aunt Gloria forgive us?

Aunt Gloria stood under the dining-room arch. "You must be starved. I'm going to fix some sausages and scrambled eggs and—"

I said, "You're going to do nothing of the sort."

"Who says? I'm fit as a fiddle and ready for love." She was over her sulking spell. She did a little jig, kicking her left foot and her right. Once upon a time Phoebe and I had been enchanted with the dance. "Do it again, just once more time." Mother never attempted the Highland Fling.

The sight of the awkward old woman was pathetic, but I was not melted.

"I am so too so," Aunt Gloria lisped. "I feel A-Number-One this morning. I don't know what got into me last night."

I kissed Mother. I said, "You're to have a nice quiet day, both of you. Anna and I are leaving now. We want to get the car unpacked. We won't be back for lunch. You aren't to fix dinner." I moved to kiss Aunt Gloria. "We'll bring back Kentucky Fried Chicken at six o'clock. Six o'clock."

Anna's eyes were wide.

141

I said, "This is your son and nephew speaking." I laughed, a kind of laugh.

Mother said, "That's perfectly fine with us. I know you're eager to get settled." Obviously my declaration had not bothered Mother. "But Gloria doesn't like Colonel Sanders. She likes Church's."

Aunt Gloria said, "I do prefer it. I read an article about Colonel Sanders. But you're not going off without your breakfast."

"We're going off without breakfast. We'll bring back Church's at six."

In the car Anna said, "That was a little scary, the dictator speech. You're going into a new period."

"What in the hell do they think we are? They could have waited."

"Calma, calma." Anna scooted closer to me. "You mustn't be upset with them."

"Aren't you? Good Lord!"

"A little, yes. What I mean is we both mustn't be upset at the same time. We've got to promise each other." Anna hugged my arm.

"My God!"

"Thou shalt not take the name of the Lord thy God in vain." Anna laughed.

"I wonder how many times I've heard that."

"As many times as it took you to stop saying, 'My God.' Remember on Military Street, before Archer was born, when . . ."

I stopped at a Walgreen's to buy a newspaper and a detailed map of Houston. I gave Anna the map. "We won't bother with the headlines."

I turned on the heater. We sat together, insulated by the sound of the engine and the warmth, separate from everybody in the whole United States.

I read the For Rent notices while Anna took notes, telephone numbers, addresses. "Hmmm, that sounds nice." "No. We're not desperate." "Very yes. Four stars." "Maybe."

I will remember that half hour as I have remembered a day in August when Mother first left us to visit Houston, when Anna and I first had our house alone together. We were young.

"Kiss me," Anna said when we had finished the list. "People always seal their pact with a kiss."

I said, "It's a nice day, isn't it?"

"It's a perfectly lovely day."

I pulled out of the parking space. A taxi driver behind us slammed on his brakes. The driver pulled beside us. He rolled down his window. I rolled down mine. He yelled, "You dumbass hillbillies."

Anna leaned past me. "My husband is quite within his rights. I'd like for you to know who is really a dumbass."

We were merry.

But the day was neither nice nor lovely.

We started with the rentals that had given addresses. We stopped every whipstitch, as Mother says, to consult the map.

Anna kept saying, "This isn't a map of Houston. This is for Hong Kong."

I considered her clever at first, then less clever: "This map is for Timbuktu"; "for Indianapolis."

We were at one of the far ends of Houston's vast limits. "We aren't even in Texas any more," she said. "This is Louisiana. We couldn't live this far out. What are we doing in Louisiana?"

I said, "Damn it," and swung the car into a McDonald's parking lot.

"I'm sure it's not my fault we're in Louisiana. Look at the map yourself."

I understand why Anna gets annoyed with my *patient* voice, but sometimes I can't muster any other voice. I said, "We are old enough, I like to think, to read a map. Together, that is."

Not without conflict, we located most of the listed addresses. Only two of them were within three miles of Bonita Avenue. One had been rented a week ago. "But the ad was in the paper today," Anna kept saying. "I don't understand why the ad was in the paper today if you rented the place a week ago." Anna was ready to argue with the proprietress, a young woman whose plastic curlers were the exact shade of her gums.

I pulled Anna back to the car. Her feelings were ruffled. I said, "We don't have time to visit with everybody in Houston. We can make friends later."

Anna said, "You make me sick."

The second possible place had been rented fifteen minutes before our arrival. The humped landlady insisted on showing it to us any-

143

how. Anna said we might as well get an idea of what we could expect. The apartment, the downstairs of a three-story house, was the kind of place we had not dared hope for: many-windowed, simply furnished. Anna said, "It's so crisp and elegant." The lonely woman said she sure would like to rent to us because we looked like such a cultured couple.

In the car I said without rancor, "You made another friend."

Anna was buoyed. "She was sweet, wasn't she? We could someday take her for a ride, maybe, with The Girls."

I said we probably would.

After seven failures we stopped for lunch at a place named Drive Inn. Anna said Mother's sentences: "We must replan our strategy; we must reorder our troops." We would cruise and reconnoiter.

Most of our friends malign fast food places. I find them as comforting as a heating pad.

No, we told each other, we would not resort to a rental agent. Yes, we would put off our telephoning until evening. We'd start at Bonita again. On the map Anna drew a careful circle around our block of Bonita.

Just as we left Drive Inn the sun came out. The sun made the world lemon-colored; the macadam of the parking lot glistened. Such phenomena often occur on leaving fast food establishments.

We stopped at every property that held a sign, including cardboard signs written in shoe polish: For Rent, For Let, Rooms, Apartment, Efficiency, even Room.

They were unfurnished. Or you had to sign a lease for a year. Or they cost eight hundred forty dollars a month. Or they were filthy— one toilet had not been flushed in the recent past. Or they were what they said they were, Room: a bed and a chair, hooks for a closet, hunched under a stained ceiling that looked unlikely to last the afternoon. "The mister isn't here," or, "The wife ain't home; she tends to such matters," or, "Those other folks are due to move out tomorrow, but seems like they can't make up their mind."

144

Anna drew larger and larger rings around Bonita, a mile-and-a-half ring, two miles, three miles.

I asked, "How in the hell do you know that's a three-mile circle?"

"I sense such things, Arch. Go back to Bonita. Check the speedometer."

"What does the speedometer have to do with it?"

"The odometer, whatever its name is."

"I don't want to go back to The Girls' house. What if they see us? Five times, ten times, riding past."

"What if they do? You're silly to expect to find anything decent in that neighborhood."

"Their place is fine. I've never seen a more pleasant apartment."

"Of course it is, but . . ."

Had we been younger we would have had a bruising argument. One of the bonuses about having been married for thirty-five years is that generally, or often, or sometimes, two people who are comfortable with each other recognize the foolishness of weary talk.

"Arch, no."

I said, "Yes. It is *Wednesday*, Hortense."

When we were first married we lived next door to an old couple named Hortense and Duke. They spent their days arguing over whether an incident had happened on a Tuesday or a Wednesday.

"It really is Tuesday, Duke."

We went to Church's for the fried chicken, slaw, mashed potatoes, rolls.

The Girls were seated in their chairs.

Aunt Gloria said, "Where in the tarnation have you been?"

"All unpacked?"

"No luck at all." I forgot to shout.

"That's nice. How very nice."

"No, Mother. No place. No luck."

"Luck?"

I shook my head.

"Poor Archie Lee."

Anna told of our day, making it into an almost funny story.

I can't figure how Anna makes Mother hear. I continue to talk to her as if I were crying out a telegram in pidgin English.

145

The table was set with the gold-band china that Mother had painted when she was in college. Anna refused to allow Aunt Gloria into the kitchen: "I am quite capable of placing ready-cooked food onto plates." Anna was sounding like The Girls. Aunt Gloria said she was the absolute limit.

Trying to copy Anna, I said that I was ready to do the dishes and no one was to get underfoot.

Aunt Gloria said, "That's sweet, Archie. I appreciate your attitude. I tell you what. We'll do it together for a while, until you get the hang of things."

At home we almost always wash the dishes within a reasonable time after a meal. Anna, energy-conscious enough to save the nation, disapproves of using the dishwasher unless we have many people for dinner. Often we leave the dishes in the drainer. Anna is not a sloppy housekeeper, but it is fair to say that she is casual. Just before we left Graham she found her favorite paring knife, which had been lost for months. It was in the flour canister.

Aunt Gloria tried to be patient with me. God knows I tried to be patient with her. I kept dreading the thought of the day when we had a real dinner to clean up after.

That night I learned many lessons, but only about silver and china. Rules for leftovers and pots and pans came later.

I list the first lessons because, I suppose, I am feeling a touch persecuted. Today has been like a long, long hike through molasses up to my kneecaps.

• Wash each piece of silver separately; dry separately and immediately; do not replace silver in silver chest immediately; leave dried silver on towel on right-hand counter to air.

• Do not slide saucers or dishes singly into their vertical compartments on the second far right-hand shelf of the top cupboards; place all dishes into their compartments simultaneously; otherwise, dishes will scratch each other. Hang cups on hooks, facing left.

• Do not use the middle-sized aluminum mixing bowl for anything, but wash it after every meal. Jeanette, one of the schoolteachers next door, a pleasant enough woman but scatterbrained, had brought camellias; she had marched right out to the kitchen and stuck the flowers into the bowl. She thought she was doing something nice, but camellias are poisonous, as every idiot ought to know. Eventually the bowl will be usable again.

• Do not use the tea towels hanging on the tea cart beside the stove; use the old tea towels hanging on the hot-water heater. When finished with drying, fold towels carefully in thirds.

• Do not use abrasives or rough cleansers on the sink or counter. Scrub your heart out.

When we finally finished cleaning up after our dinner from Church's, Aunt Gloria gave me two kisses and several pats. In the living room she declared that I was a great help. "You've never seen a faster learner."

I wasn't planning to say anything offensive even if Anna hadn't glowered at me. I said, "I'll be doing it by myself in no time."

Aunt Gloria said, "We'll see," punching my ribs with her elbow.

Anna went into Aunt Gloria's room to telephone the list. Mother and Aunt Gloria took catnaps while I roared little anecdotes. Hoarse, I suggested television. The Girls said they had rather hear me talk.

Friday was a replica of Thursday, except Aunt Gloria replaced the china with paper plates. "It'll be easier on Archie Lee until he gets used to things."

Anna and I loathe paper plates and what they do to food.

Saturday was Thursday and Friday, except our circling of Bonita Avenue had increased another four miles.

"It's time to get the chicken," Anna said. In the dash light her face looked old.

"Let's get the hell home, to our real home, to Graham."

"We can't, Arch. You know that. We came to help them."

I said, "Shit." Anna is offended by the word. Surprisingly, it is a word Mother considers legitimate in times of total exasperation. It is a word her father, the paragon of all virtues, sanctioned. Childish, I said, "Double shit."

147

We were at the corner of Alabama and Pullen.

"Wait. Stop! Arch!"

I slammed on the brakes, making the car almost slide into a parked truck.

"What's the matter with you?"

"There. Back up. Back up about six houses."

I backed up, too irritated to speak.

A rectangle of cement block squatted in the dark rain. It was a residential street, like Bonita, but there in the middle of the block crouched the Skyview. A sign, no larger than a card table, lit by a single bulb, said: Motel Skyview. Efficiencies. By Week or Month. The letters were gray.

"We've been here before, Anna."

"Maybe not. Maybe we thought it was just a regular motel. Maybe we passed it when we were being choosy. I have a feeling, Arch."

Already in Houston Anna had experienced at least a dozen feelings. I do not trust Anna's feelings, but I admit them. "Look, it's two stories. They have lots of places."

I asked Anna how she knew. I asked her how a two-story building could give the impression of squatting.

Anna said, "They have some kind of law in Houston against zoning. It doesn't matter."

Before I complimented her logic, before I had stopped the engine, Anna was out of the car and running up the walk past the sign. I turned off the motor. I thought of staying in the car. I got out clumsily, swearing. I locked the car. I wondered how many times I had locked the car within the past three days. You're in Sin City now, boy, I told myself. You're a goddamned Good Samaritan in Sin City.

I patted the hood of the car as if to wish good luck to somebody or something. The act was like praying. I was more desperate than I was willing to admit.

The Skyview is two double layers of picture windows and glass doors, fourteen upstairs and fourteen down, looking at each other across a cobbled courtyard. Two ailanthus trees stand together in the center of the courtyard, holding each other up. A sign, gray on gray again, nailed to one of the trees says, Manager Apt. 15. The second layer of Skyview is reached by a curved iron stairway. In rain, the wayfarer must hold to the railing or he will fall back to the courtyard, flat on his ass.

People are always falling on their asses in Archer's books.

The applicant will slip even if he is holding tightly to the railings with both hands.

Anna stood at a lighted door on the second level. "Here, Arch. Come, Arch. I want you to meet Darling." I could have been a backward dog at obedience school. "And she does have a place, a just-vacated place."

I was out of breath from the climb. "How do you do, Miss Darling."

Darling and I shook hands. She had a strong handshake. "That's my first name. That's what my mama named me. Everybody asks about it. I don't mind." Darling's laugh started as a kind of sneeze, then rose an octave. "She's still living, but in Canada. I ain't seen her for years."

She was a vast young woman, no taller than Anna. I wondered idly if it would take two or three of Anna to make one of Darling.

Darling's hair, a lovely auburn, hung loose to her vast waist. She wore tight red shorts; her brassiere, blue, was an ineffective sling, a casual hammock for her large breasts. I was so tired I was afraid I would join her laughter.

"You don't mind if we have a look?" Anna was being the gracious lady.

I said, to my own surprise, "We're pretty goddamned tired of looking."

"Arch!"

I couldn't have said anything better. Darling was all smiles. She patted our arms. I had established a norm of language to Darling's liking. She was suddenly our friend, not the landlady.

She pressed her forefinger against her lips. "Now where in the hell did I put those damn keys?"

Darling's apartment, what I could see behind her head, was ablaze with plastic flowers and lamps and figurines. A color television roared cartoons. A baby cried. "Oh, yes, I was just changing Junior. You'll excuse me, won't you kindly?"

A disco light sprackled the room. For a moment I thought I had lost my sight. The pillows on the couch were purple, orange, yellow, blinding white.

Darling returned. A baby cried again.

149

Darling called over her shoulder, "Charlie, you tend to that kid. Charlie, you hear me?" She laughed her frightening laugh. "He just got off from work. He's in the bathroom. Charlie's my awful wedded husband. You all just follow me."

Darling did not close the door behind us. She said, "You can't believe how long that man can take in the bathrom. But he's crazy about that little girl."

"Girl?" Anna asked.

"She's named after me."

The crying stopped.

Anna said, "Shouldn't you . . . don't you need a wrap?"

Darling said she was hot-blooded. Charlie was just the opposite. He'd keep the heat on high in summer if she let him. Charlie was crazy. The apartments were heated good, too good. And they were quiet, real good insulation. "There ain't a lot of room, but enough room. Me and Charlie got three rooms because I'm the manager."

She was a good salesman.

"I'm crazy about Skyview. I love making people happy. Here we be. Number seven, lucky number seven."

Darling had difficulty opening the door. "If Charlie don't get around to fixing those doors, I'm going to kill him." She smiled at us over her shoulder. "Looka there. We got lights at every corner. They go on automatic and turn off automatic. Dusk to dawn, as they say. But they're set for September. If Charlie don't get around to . . ."

She shook the doorknob. She said, "Fuck it," and the door opened. "Excuse my French. You just step right in."

Darling flipped the light switch. Nothing happened. "Oh, golly. But you can get an idea of what it's like. Those bastards that just moved out! I'm a good judge of character, but I sure missed on those bastards." Darling stood in the center of the dark room, cradling her breasts. "I couldn't let you have it until Monday. Charlie's off Sunday. I want you to be happy. I'd do anything in the world for people like youse. But I wouldn't let pigs set foot in the place like it is, even clean pigs."

Anna said, "Careful. Compliments go to our heads."

150

I told myself to remind Anna that she should never be very funny in front of Darling.

I was assuming we had already taken the place.

In the shadows I could make out a studio couch under the window, a corner table, another studio couch against the wall. There was a dinette table and four chairs in the left-hand corner of the room; in the right-hand corner, a bar with two stools. The bar was lung height on me, shoulder height on Anna.

"Kitchen's on the other side of the bar. The stove's not much, but the frigerator's brand spankin' new. Dishes and so forths. Everything's furnished. But no TV. The old bitch who owns the place won't buy none. The colored girl in number eighteen's going to leave hers, at least that's what she said."

"May I try this light switch?" Anna stood at the large opening in the back of the room.

"Sure, honey. But you know damn well those turds took ever light bulb in the house. That's the way with turds. I sure missed on them. That hole in the wall. That's the vanity. Bath on your right, closet on the left."

The alcove screamed light.

Anna and I jumped at the sight of ourselves in the mirror over the vanity counter. We looked like old clothespin dolls. The mirror covered the wall above the counter that held a filthy washbasin. Four roaches, two on either side of the basin, raced and disappeared.

Darling was behind us. "Those goddamned bugs. I'll get 'em. They're not as bad as they was in Florida, thank God. Charlie and me lived in Florida once. But they're all over Houston—River Oaks, too. That's the ritzy section—not that I would know personal." Darling was noisily amused at her little joke.

The bathroom light worked. Five roaches inhabited the tub. Anna flicked off the light. "And over here. What a nice big closet!"

"The bugs. The roaches. They're manageable?" I asked Darling in the mirror.

"You gotta keep after 'em. I wouldn't lie to you. I hate the sons of bitches. Also there ain't no telephone. But you can give every-

151

body my number. Or you could have a phone put in. It won't take but a year or two." Darling's laughter made us all jump, even Darling.

Anna said, "It will be a relief not to have a telephone. We don't know anybody anyhow."

"Tell you God's truth, I love telephones. It's awful nice to know somebody's out there. I think Charlie's getting me a new one for Christmas, a Snoopy."

I did not know what she meant. I said, "I don't think we'll be bothering you. Except for matters of flood and death."

Darling considered me very humorous.

Anna said, "The vanity counter, Arch. It will be a marvelous place for you to write."

Darling let go of her breasts. "Write? My God, you don't mean you're a writer?"

"My wife exaggerates. We're here to take care of my mother and aunt. Really, Anna—"

"My God, I can't wait to tell Charlie. He'll have a double duck-fit. He reads all the time. That's what he does in the bathroom. My God! I've had a feeling all day. All day I've had this feeling, like something important was going to happen."

I said, "Anna has feelings too."

Anna and I raised eyebrows at each other. We had made a decision. We said, "All right," almost at the same time. I do not know which of the *all rights* was weaker, but we spoke together.

"I'm mighty glad." Darling looked capable of crying. "I hate to say this to folks like youse, but it's cash in advance. The old bitch wouldn't let me take a check from Jesus Christ."

In the dark I fumbled for my billfold. "Not until you move in, honeys."

Darling walked with us to the car. "I forgot to tell you, there's a parking lot in the basement. You get to it by the alley off Washington."

"A parking lot, Arch. Imagine that." Anna told Darling to get back in the house before she caught her death of cold.

"I'll get those son-of-a-bitchin' bugs," Darling called to us.

We did not speak until Church's. "I didn't mean to annoy you, about the writing. But you must, Arch."

"Okay. That's okay."

"We'll just pay for one week. We can stand anything for a week. It may be just fine."

We were forty minutes late with dinner for The Girls. They were not particularly annoyed with us. They were pleased we had found a place. Now we could have proper time for visiting, they said.

The chicken, slaw, rolls, potatoes were delicious.

"Now what's our schedule for tomorrow?" Aunt Gloria pushed back her plate. "There are a few little items I just have to get."

"Tomorrow's Sunday, Gloria." Mother looked hurt.

"I just have to, Donna. We're low on butter and toilet paper. The better the day, the better the deed. I'll put off the real shopping until Monday. Tomorrow we'll have breakfast together. Anna and I will go out and get a few little things. You and Archie can have a nice visit. You can watch your church service together. Donna's preacher does his sermon on the TV. After lunch we'll have our naps. Archie and Anna can disappear for an hour or so. They need their privacy, a little rest period. Then maybe we'll take a little ride, Donna Dale, if you feel up to it."

The morning and the evening were the first three and a half days.

We followed Aunt Gloria's schedule from Sunday through Wednesday, the longest four-day period of my life.

We were at The Girls' apartment by eight o'clock. They sat in their chairs in their lavender and yellow robes Anna had made for them two Christmases ago.

Anna cooked field-hand breakfasts. After a blessing, muttered by me or intoned by Mother, The Girls took their pills and vitamins, which Aunt Gloria had placed in the Dresden salt dishes. Then The Girls fell upon their food. Anna was the best cook they had ever eaten after, they said. They were gaining weight, they said.

Anna managed to burn the grits, or the bacon, or the eggs, or the toast—The Girls preferred oven toast. By Wednesday she was burning everything, all day.

Anna apologized profusely. "We'll replace the skillet and the saucepan. I don't know what's got into me."

Aunt Gloria said she was not to worry. "I know I'm silly about pots and pans. It's just that I love them. I buy them the way other ladies buy jewelry. They've just been used a few times. I almost never use them."

Mother said she relished a little burned taste.

We moved into Skyview during our rest period on Monday afternoon.

The apartment glittered, as much as it was capable of glittering.

Darling had done a monumental job of cleaning. The frayed velveteen draperies, the color of dried blood, had been dry-cleaned. The vanity basin and the tub, save for the rust marks of long-leaking faucets, gleamed. There was a new garbage can and a new wastebasket, scarlet; a new scarlet dish drainer; a new lampshade decorated with Charlie Brown and Snoopy.

Darling helped us unload the car. She blushed at our compliments until her face and neck were the color of her T-shirt.

I said, "How can we unpack so quickly when it took me so long to pack?"

"We didn't have Darling."

Darling pressed her hands over her face and laughed helplessly.

We were early getting back to The Girls.

"Right on schedule," Aunt Gloria said. "I'm making a list for tomorrow. The bulb in Donna Dale's magnifying glass has burned out. And the mixer rubber has been faulty for over a year, and there's a real sale at Handy Andy's. It was advertised on television. You saw it, Donna."

"Handy Andy is miles away, Gloria. You'll wear Anna out."

"And we're almost out of stamps."

I said, "I'll drive you tomorrow."

"You're here to visit with your mother. Anna and I are the shoppers. You hush, Arch."

Those scheduled days, I visited awhile with Mother after the front door had closed behind the shoppers. It is a pattern I have continued through assorted days. Before engaging my dishes I give Anna time to sashay back into the house to fetch Aunt Gloria's purse or gloves, the shopping list, coupons that have come in the mail.

Doing the dishes has become a positive pleasure, a game more complicated and satisfactory than chess. I scour the burned pots and pans until I can see myself in them. When washing the gray enamel saucepan, I do not place the pan directly into the sink: I have learned to place the bottom of the pan on a plastic ice-cream top; otherwise, the gray enamel pan leaves ugly marks in the sink. There are no marks in my sink. I remember to wash the middle-sized aluminum bowl.

At home in Graham I would be shoveling snow. I would be trying to quiet Ray Fletcher's yammering about Dr. White and his book list. The telephone would be ringing off the wall. That salesman from Columbus would be settling down for a wearisome sales pitch about his T-shirts and shorts.

My visits with Mother are pleasant. She dictates letters to Phoebe, our children, friends in Kentucky. I am impressed by her letters; they are the meaning of "friendly" letters. She is concerned about the people she writes to; everything is fine with us, her health is improving by leaps and bounds; what a marvelous time we are having.

But she tires quickly.

I read to her. We have finished *Elizabeth and Her German Garden*. Next we start *Enchanted April*. I know she misses a great deal, but she never asks me to reread a passage. She sits, smiling, her hand cupped to her ear. My stomach hurts from pulling it in to shout as loudly as I am able.

"Thank you so much, Arch. That's very interesting. And how wonderful it is to get those letters off my mind."

Occasionally there are telephone calls, from Trixie or other church ladies. Mother's bedside telephone has a cord long enough to reach into the living room. She chats for quite a while. I write notes to Ray Fletcher and Archer and Charlotte (Please Forward).

"It's strange, Arch, but I think I hear better on the telephone than in normal conversations."

"I think you're hearing better all the time."

"How's that?"

The shopping always takes longer than expected, by an hour or two.

Some days I have fixed lunch on trays—soup, toasted sandwiches, the congealed salad Anna has made. I am proud of myself. Better still, I have our dishes washed and put away before Aunt Gloria and Anna return.

While insisting that she eats only two meals a day, Aunt Gloria devours Anna's lunches. "Ain't we got fun!" Aunt Gloria says at least once a meal. She says, "Family! There's nothing like a family."

My sixty-year-old kneecaps still tense when she uses the word *family*. She makes it the juiciest word in the language.

For the first days The Girls followed their old habit of naps at 2 P.M. Anna and I went back to Skyview and collapsed. We lay on the marshmallow beds and told each other on The Girls.

Our queen-sized bed at home is as firm as a sidewalk. At Skyview we first tried putting the mattresses on the floor, then we slept, or tried to sleep, on the floor itself, daring roaches to attack us. I had spoken to Darling about the beds. Darling looked hurt. "They're the best damn beds in the whole goddamned place. I saw to it you'd get the best beds." I thanked her profusely. Mollified, she said I was as welcome as the flowers of spring.

"And do you know, Arch, there's almost nothing to wash: nightgowns, some towels, the tea towels you never use, sheets? We smooth and fold and refold—Aunt Gloria made me refold a tea towel three times. And do you know, Arch, Mil irons everything? She gets up at six o'clock to starch and iron, even the bath towels. Aunt Gloria says it makes Mil feel necessary. I could die over them."

"It's all right." We held hands across the corner table, under the Peanuts lamp. "We mustn't let ourselves be as sad as we are able. That's one of your sayings."

Wednesday afternoon we made love.

And then we told each other that The Girls were really remarkable, and we were getting along splendidly. Anna said, "Poor Aunt Gloria. She's been stuck in the house with Mil forever. She adores shopping, just looking at *things*. It's the least I can do to drive her around to look at *things*."

I said, "We've got to protect ourselves."

"You're right, Arch. There's no point in your sitting with Mil every morning. She's never needed a sitter before when Aunt Gloria went out. And you haven't written a word. You promised."

"I did nothing of the sort."

"Promise now. You're promising now."

I said, "Anna, Anna." I like the sound of her name.

157

Since the first day we settled into Skyview, Mother has felt up to taking a little ride.

Getting The Girls into the car is an ordeal. Mother's walker, an aluminum contraption of bars, handles, and legs, is too tall for her. Getting down the three porch steps is a major achievement. "Wait. Wait a minute. I'm all right. I'm just fine." Mother perspires even when the air is harsh. "Fine. One more. One more step."

At the car door Mother hands me the walker, turns herself slowly, holding to me and the doorframe. She takes one step backward and collapses into the seat. She is able to hoist her left foot to the floorboard; I lift her right foot for her.

Only once has she said, "It's so humiliating." Generally she says, "Splendid. Splendid, Arch."

Anna helps, shovels rather, Aunt Gloria into the back seat. As if in sympathy with Mother, Aunt Gloria often has spells of trembling, weaving, and staggering. It is difficult to get her settled, but she never allows me to help. "Anna will do it, Arch. She knows how."

I place the walker in the trunk of the car.

"And off we go," Mother says. "Hoorah, hooray."

Aunt Gloria says, "Is everybody's door locked? Arch, you haven't locked your door. You're in Houston, don't forget. Sometimes those fellows just open the doors and drag you out."

During our little rides I have often remembered Mother's seventy-fifth birthday. It doesn't seem very long ago; it was during their summer visit.

Mother had walked into town and back, a matter of three miles, "just for a little airing. A woman should have a little airing on her seventy-fifth birthday."

I was standing in the front yard when she returned. It was late afternoon. I stood under the oak tree. In the June haze I watched a figure approach, a woman. She moved beautifully, dispelling the haze. The woman did not walk; she glided, ordering the afternoon.

It was my mother.

I was smiling. My face almost hurt with smiling.

158   The Girls prefer late-afternoon rides of an hour or two, through traffic to little side roads that are identical to one another: the same flat fields, the same ranch houses on whose lawns parade large plastic

ducks and small plastic flamingos. Occasionally Aunt Gloria spots several cattle egrets or a sparrow hawk. Mother pretends to see them, but she is looking in the wrong direction.

Coming and going we pass Skyview. Always we suggest that The Girls come in to see our place. Mother says, "Another time. We want very much to see where you dwell and have your being, but another time." Anna and I ponder over why they have never felt up to entering Skyview.

Twice they have met Darling. Both times she was standing by the Skyview sign; both times she wore her red shorts and blue brassiere. I stopped the car and called to her. Darling rushed to us. The Girls lowered their windows slowly. Darling has shaken their hands vigorously. "Your health is better, I like to trust," and, "I think the world and all of your family," she has said both times.

Both times as we drove away Anna said, "She's a jewel, really."

Aunt Gloria said, "In the very rough. If jewel she be."

Mother said, "She's the limit. I'm glad you can tolerate her."

We have not bothered to argue with The Girls.

The Girls like for the little rides to conclude with a sunset. They are devoted to sunsets. "That is beauty beyond description," one of them says, and the other describes it, naming the shape and shade of every color. They do not mind that the sunsets occur during rush hour traffic.

And then there is the getting out of the car and into the apartment. Dinner, another banquet. The dishwashing. The conversation.

Back to Skyview, to fall, generally, into our separate beds.

One of the nights Anna said, "What you call life is . . . what you call a life is after it's all finished." She was crying.

But we have not often talked seriously to each other in Houston.

We are consumed with minutiae, the handling of half hours that make a day.

Time stretches long.

Anna said she could not remember Graham. I said we had been born and reared in Skyview. We have made up quotations for bumper stickers. IF YOU WANT TIME TO STAND STILL, COME TO HOUSTON. CRAZY ABOUT IMMORTALITY? HOUSTON!

159

It was probably a Thursday morning. We were rushing as usual, as speedily as our aching backs allowed. Anna stopped on the thirtieth stroke of her ritual hair brushing. "Today we are being liberated. Today we do something about those beds."

Anna had threatened to do something about the beds even before we had slept in them. I said, "Okay. Right. You look a touch haggard."

"Thanks. And likewise. I'm looking like a raccoon. And you're going to start writing."

"We'll see."

"I mean it. We've got to have something to show for being here. We don't want to go crazy. I'm burning more pans every day. I'm getting a little crazy, and I'm better put together than you are."

I told her that if she had a flaw it was modesty. We hugged each other. And then we stumbled down to the garage, the Black Pit of Egypt.

That morning's breakfast was pancakes, many of them unburned, and little sausages, several of them unburned. Aunt Gloria, slavering butter on her fifth pancake, said, "I've gained four pounds. I'm going on a diet tomorrow." She said, "There's nothing like a family," although the entire meal's conversation had been devoted to vilifying a couple of first cousins who live in Cleveland, who never wrote except for a little scratch on their printed Christmas cards, who considered themselves "something," although both of them were married to barbers, not that there was anything wrong with barbers.

Aunt Gloria said, "Now, what's our exact schedule for today?"

In a small voice Anna said, "Arch and I are going to town."

Aunt Gloria said, "I did the most awful thing Monday. I absolutely overlooked Donna Dale's sheets and towels. And the curtains in both our rooms are a disgrace. It will be lovely to have clean curtains for Christmas. Mama always did. Remember, Donna Dale? She had a little poem about it, something she cut out of a newspaper:

> For Christmas Day,
> Come what may,
> Be very certain
> You have clean curtains."

"Arch and I have to go to town. We have to get bed boards." Anna swallowed hard. "Bed boards for the beds."

I wasn't really paying attention. I said without thinking, "I thought we were going during the rest period."

Anna looked very small, and vulnerable, and tired. "Oh?"

I said, "We're going this morning. Right away. We'll drop the laundry off on the way to town." I spoke loudly. Anna flinched.

"No, Arch. We'll stay with it. You're supposed to stay with it. I'll fold it right. I'll do it . . . just right."

Aunt Gloria rattled her coffee cup on its saucer. "We aren't going to allow you to do our dirty linen."

Mother said, "You toddle right out of here."

Anna was almost in charge of herself. "And something else. Arch must get to his writing. Now that he has time."

I tried to catch her eye, but she wouldn't look at me.

"What a good idea," Mother said. "He can just spread out on the dining room table and write to his heart's content. We'll be quiet as mice, won't we, Gloria?"

"No, Milly. He has it set up at our . . ."

We have both had trouble in naming where we live.

Mother said, "Place? Apartment?"

"At our apartment place." Anna nodded. "There's that vanity counter; it means to be a desk. He can't concentrate with people around."

Mother said, "I can't wait to read what he writes. Archie Lee is capable, and he finishes what he starts."

"Oh, Mother."

I was almost overwhelmed with the four of us: Aunt Gloria, to whom a trip to the laundromat was a festival; Mother, who was determined to pretend that degenerate time was an endless ribbon; vulnerable, accommodating Anna. I was sorry for myself on general principles. I washed the dishes while Anna took down the curtains and Aunt Gloria gathered up what stray items she could find. Even with the curtains there was barely a pillowcase of laundry.

161

It was a splendid day, all day was a splendid day.

The laundromat was full of congenial human beings. We folded everything perfectly.

Penney's was having a sale on skillets and saucepans exactly like the utensils Anna had terminally burned.

The man at the lumberyard couldn't have been kinder.

We sneaked the two boards into No. 7 without Darling's seeing us. We didn't want to hurt her feelings. We giggled, almost dropping the boards back down the steps of the Black Pit.

I've read that people give up giggling after thirty-five.

You can read anything.

That day was spring. We were out of school on a day we had been expecting an arithmetic test.

We had just finished installing the bed boards and remaking the beds when Darling rapped at the door. She wore Junior in a carrier on her back. Junior is a replica of Darling, the same auburn hair, the same blue eyes. Junior smiled and gurgled, reaching over her mother's shoulders to Anna. Anna insists that Junior is the most adorable child in the universe. Perhaps she is.

Darling stood on one leg, then the other. She said she was just checking up on us. How was Mama and Auntie getting along? What was we doing home this time of day?

Anna explained that we were on a new schedule. "We'll be here—home—more often. The Girls are getting along well."

We stood at the door, our own arms folded. We complimented the absence of roaches. Darling said she was sure glad to hear everything was hunky-dory, and wasn't it a nice day for a change.

Anna cooed at Junior and patted her cheek. And then she said, as if to Junior, "Arch will be writing every morning. Maybe every afternoon."

Darling said, "Oh, my God. A masterpiece, I'm sure."

That afternoon I settled down to write.

I wrote such paragraphs as:

Your head looks totally bald from the front and you need a haircut.
Your hair is the color of wet cement. You have a small nose.

I wrote:

He has deep lines from the sides of his nose down below his lips,
which are rather full. He does not look Swedish.

When he presses his hands, his fingers, up against his cheek-
bones, he looks Oriental. But everybody does. He doesn't look like anybody named Narcissus. His wife is a beautiful woman, but she doesn't
know it.

Once that afternoon, when I lifted my eyes from the typewriter
keys to the mirror, I saw Darling at the window, her hands cupped
around her eyes. I waved into the mirror. Darling and Junior waved
back.

She was not spying, just checking. I did not for a fantasizing
male moment think that Darling yearned for my aging body.

If I were in one of Archer's books, I would welcome Darling into
the apartment. In three minutes we would be on the floor together,
panting together for two or three pages. Darling would race back to
her apartment only seconds before Anna returned from The Girls.
Darling and I would plot against Charlie's life. Perhaps we would

push him over the balcony. Anna would take care of him in the hospital.

I wrote:

> My face in the mirror is not the face I saw yesterday before I started writing. It is interesting, but not very, to imagine tomorrow's face.

Along about five o'clock I placed the new scarlet wastebasket on the top of the bar counter. I crumpled each of my twenty pages of offensive paragraphs into tight balls. Seated at the vanity I tried to toss each of the balls into the basket. I moved slowly, taking careful aim. I hit three times. I emptied the basket and tried again. Seven goals. The third practice period was three again. It was time to walk to The Girls' for dinner.

I said, "Sorry I'm a little late. I've been writing."

Anna said, "Oh, Arch, I can't wait."

When we got back to Skyview, Anna seated herself primly at the dinette table. "I feel like a bride."

"You have no reason to."

"Come on, Arch. Where is it?"

"You want to read aloud?"

"That's the plan, isn't it?"

I handed her the wastebasket.

She removed my paper wads carefully. She smoothed them out carefully. "The manuscript is not in the best condition." She pursed her lips.

"You can't have everything." I bit my lips to keep from laughing.

Anna began to intone the words, modeling herself, I suppose, after the lady poets who often give readings at Graham College.

She got through the passages about my hair and my face before she collapsed. "It's interesting, Arch." She put her hands over her mouth. Her laughter broke through her hands.

I was actually roaring. I felt that I had produced the most hilarious prose of any century.

In Archer's novels people are always rocking in each other's arms. We rocked in each other's arms.

164

Later, in our beds, exhausted from laughing, Anna said, "I guess people really could die laughing."

I said, "All these years I've been a liar. I'd rather be anything in the world than a writer."

Anna moved in her bed. She was turning on the lamp. "Look at me, Arch."

I said, "That light's blinding me."

"You promised." Anna is a great one for the sanctity of promises.

I said, "Okay. I'll tell on us." I was still laughing, but I had stopped being amused.

Anna snickered herself into sleep.

I did not sleep that night.

I am not telling the truth.

I slept often that night, dreaming all of the frightening dreams, the fall, the chase, the figure waiting to pounce from the black dark. I tried to shout. I pulled my stomach in to shout, but no sound came. I was trying to warn somebody—Anna or Archer or Charlotte or Mother. I was trying to warn Junior whose blue eyes were a doll's eyes; somebody had gouged out Junior's eyes.

Anna was leaning over me. "Arch, honey. You're all right. You just had a little nightmare. Take off that wet pajama top. You're all right, Arch."

A slim strip of light showed between the dark drapes. We were at a place named Skyview in a town named Houston, Texas.

"I yelled, didn't I?"

"Not really. Just a kind of loud grunt. You haven't had a nightmare forever. Here. Get into these dry pajamas."

I slept again, to dream again, the fall, the chase. I was trying to save somebody from something.

Anna was dressed and tiptoeing to the door when I woke. "Ssssh, Arch. Go back to sleep. Sleep in today."

"I had a nightmare, didn't I?"

"A little one. I'll be home for lunch probably. We're on a new schedule, which means no schedule. It's called weaning. You have a good day."

"I'll have the kind of day I damn well please." I was quoting Archer.

Anna laughed and blew me two more kisses.

165

After my breakfast of grapefruit, coffee, and a toasted peanut butter sandwich, I walked to the grocery on Alabama and bought my newspaper.

I sat at the typewriter and read the paper. A policeman had been killed, three girls raped. One of the girls was ten years old. Iran still held the hostages—I recalled that the hostages had appeared in the nightmare. Somebody had given a speech at a Rotary Club on World War III. A cat named Beasley had walked from Wichita to Houston.

I kept being distracted by people who passed in the mirror. I was distracted by my own face, even though it was the same face I had seen yesterday.

I closed the draperies, felt smothered; opened them, felt like an exhibitionist; closed them halfway, missed the sun on my back; opened them again.

Every morning the sun investigates the whole room. It is good to sit at the vanity counter, warmed by the sun.

Before I got around to writing I took a couple of towels from the bathroom and tried to wedge them in the crevice between the top of the mirror and the wall. They fell as soon as I sat down. My face glared ugly at me. I tried again. The right-hand towel fell. A man with half a face glared at me.

I found Scotch tape in Anna's sewing box. The newspaper held nicely to the mirror.

I was sitting on a barstool drinking my fourth cup of coffee when I realized Darling was standing at the opened door. She held her hands behind her back. Her mouth was pursed, like Anna's when she was awaiting her first reading. Darling fluttered her pale eyelashes. I went to the door.

"I don't never stop when I seen you writing. Not never."

"That is very considerate of you, Darling." Darling's language is always surprising. She is generally most ungrammatical when she is being most ladylike.

She brought her right hand from behind her. Slowly she wagged her forefinger in front of her nose. "You sure put one over on me."

I found Darling the Coy considerably less attractive than the natural Darling who don't make no bones about nothing. Also, I was thinking about writing. I was remembering the day Mother made her first trip to Houston, leaving Anna and me alone in the house for the first time.

"I'm sorry, Darling. I hadn't intended to put one over on you."

Slowly—all of Darling's motions were very slow that morning—she brought her left hand to her front. She held a book. "You could of told me. Anna or you could of told me. Anna should of told me."

I said, "A book. That's a book."

"You rascal." Darling showed all of her teeth. "My God, I almost had a conniption. There I was, rolling Junior through the park, and there I was smack in front of the library. And I had this here feeling. It just come over me. I left Junior on the sidewalk, and I took me up them steps."

It was Archer's book, of course, the second one, named *The Cast*. I said, "You've made a mistake. That book happens to be—"

"Wait, let me tell you. I had this feeling and I went up them steps, and the lady was nice as pie, and I asked her if she knowed about you, and she reached over and picked up this book—somebody had just brung it back. I told her I knowed you, I was your landlady, and you could of knocked her over with a feather."

I assume I do not blush. But I felt as if I were blushing. "Darling, that's not—"

"And I brung it home. That was yesterday. I almost ain't been asleep, I ain't done nothing but read. I ain't stopped except to poke some food at Junior and Charlie. I'm about wore out. And I'm here to pay you a compliment. Although before God I wouldn't of guessed you wrote that book. You've sure had some experiences."

"My son. My son is a writer. He wrote *The Cast*. I couldn't have written it, before God."

"That's your name, ain't it?" Darling swallowed hard. "Archer Baxter?"

I had never heard Darling say my name before. From the first night she has said *Anna* easily, but I have been *you*, or *him*, or *the mister*. I said, "We share a name."

Darling looked as if I had slapped her. "You don't know what a disappointment."

"The picture on the back. That's Archer."

"I thought maybe it's an old book. He looks like you a little."

"I'm sorry to disappoint."

167

"But you're writing a book, ain't you? That wasn't no lie."

"I'm writing."

"That's a little help. I'd sure hate to have to go back and tell that lady I was a goddamned liar."

I gave her what comfort I could. "There's possibly no need."

"I'll think about it." Darling was peering over my shoulder at the vanity counter. I had left the light on.

I said, "I appreciate your dropping by. Archer will be pleased."

Darling said, "That is sure a funny way to read the newspaper, if I may say so."

We have always thought of ourselves as fairly private people.

We excuse our consuming curiosity about our neighbors here by saying that Skyview and Bonita Avenue are the world: human beings should be interested in the world.

We have worried and occasionally lost some sleep over the hostages, the economy, oil, gold, Ronald Reagan, floods and earthquakes. But we have not worried so much as we would have at home. Home is a more stable place for national and international worrying.

We nod and speak to everybody we pass in the courtyard or at the garbage cans in the Black Pit. Everybody speaks to us except for the elegant young couple in No. 11, who wear huge dark glasses and matching clothes and probably never speak to each other.

There are an affable man and wife and two little boys from New Zealand. The little boys play with a Frisbee in the courtyard every afternoon.

There is a handsome black girl in No. 18, a dancer, we have decided, who stays home all day, disappears, and returns long after midnight.

There are Minnie and Mickey, a somber couple who scurry past our window every morning at seven-thirty, scurry back at five. For three days a young girl, twelve or thirteen, scurried with them. Anna concluded that the Mices are white-slave traffickers who work schoolyards. The young girl was a reject.

A youngish man in a wheelchair and an old lady rarely close their drapes in No. 3. The old lady wears an apron; her hands are always occupied, knitting, sewing, snapping beans. The young man smiles. On the sill of their picture window stand seven small trophies, three gold, four silver, figures of athletes who swing tennis rackets and golf clubs. We wave and nod to the Trophy People.

We do not openly question Darling about the inhabitants of Sky-view, but we snatch at every crumb of information she lets drop. Neither of us is very good at quizzing. When we meet a friend swathed in bandages we never ask, "What happened?" Anna says I begin to discuss Japanese beetles, which is not exactly true, but true enough. She says that everybody will eventually get around to telling you what you're curious about if you're quietly curious.

Darling is not much help. When we pose subtle wonderings about the other tenants, Darling says, "I dunno. They pay their rent." Anna says that Darling is too busy to concentrate on more than two tenants at a time and we, unworthy though we be, have won the attention prize.

We are meeting Archer at the airport on Sunday afternoon, December 23, at four o'clock.

Aunt Gloria began a shopping list as soon as we left the telephones.

Anna said, "He's a light eater. Mark was the ravenous one. Anyhow, the refrigerator's bulging, and he won't be here until—"

"Boys are always hungry. You should know that, Anna."

Darling is also beside herself that Archer is coming. Fortunately, the two men in No. 8, the ones who wear porkpie hats and lumber jackets and leave at ten o'clock in the morning, are checking out on the twenty-second. For all we know, Darling is kicking them out to prepare a place for Archer.

I have been thinking of Mark.

Perhaps I will allow myself to write about Mark tomorrow.

Tonight will be the eighth night Anna has read to me.

Last night when Anna finished reading she said, "Don't make things sad for yourself, for ourselves. And don't write about Charlotte. I can't imagine why that child doesn't call us."

Sounding like Mother, I said, "I have no intention of making things sad. And I'm not writing about Charlotte. And we're not worrying about her."

Today is Monday. I am fond of Mondays, although I have never gone around saying so, not wanting to offend most of the people I know who speak regularly of Gloomy Mondays and Monday Blues.

I have not realized until recently that I am fond of Mondays because of Mark. I am surprised and pleased to recognize my inheritances from the children. Last night I told Anna that I had probably inherited more from Archer and Mark and Charlotte than they have inherited from me.

Anna said, "I've been thinking about Mark, too."

I quoted Mark, " 'Oh boy, a whole new week. A birthday and a Monday.' Remember?"

Anna said, "And Archer and Mark would argue. Markie never would agree that Sunday was the first day of the week."

I had forgotten. It was a pleasure to remember.

Anna had wanted to have a party for Mark's twelfth birthday, inviting every boy in his room—Miss Hattie's class. Mark said he'd rather not. "Why don't us guys go to Lake Baldwin? We haven't been there in a month of Sundays."

Mark delighted in phrases like *a month of Sundays, fine as frog's hair, crooked as a corkscrew.* And after he was in bed he always called, "Sleep tight; don't let the bedbugs bite." I could make a litany of Mark's sayings. "Knock, knock. Who's there?"

Archer thought Lake Baldwin was a good idea; Charlotte, only four, was not yet old enough to consider any family gathering too barfy for endurance.

I reminded Anna of her saying that for mothers, every birthday party was more exhausting than any birth.

"I know, I know. I really loathe birthday parties. But you should have something to remember on your twelfth birthday."

"But he wants to go to Lake Baldwin."

"Sure. Okay. Marvelous."

The five of us set out at eleven in the morning. Mark got to choose his place in the car—the window seat up front. Mark had chosen the menu. Anna had fixed lima beans in the hot thermos, four-bean salad and sauerkraut in the cold thermoses; peanut-butter-and-bleu-cheese sandwiches; the ice chest held two cartons of Cokes; a boxed chocolate cake said, "Happy Returns, Mark, Old Man."

We were Protestants conducting a bar mitzvah.

Anna told me to put the food in the trunk of the car while she rounded up towels and bathing suits. I put the ice chest on the front seat, accessible for the drive. The telephone rang. It was a girl from The Bookstore, some question I have forgotten.

We had an old Ford then, tan, which broke down on bridges— only a few bridges, but enough to give itself a reputation. I admired that car. We fitted into it exactly.

We arrived at Lake Baldwin about noon. I had forgotten my wristwatch. I was pleased with having forgotten. Anna and the children have never worn watches. They sense time.

It was the finest September day I can remember in a life of fine September days. It was a gold day. A few impossibly white clouds postured around the sky, proving how blue a September day could be. The dogwood leaves had already turned dark pink and mahogany, the sumac burned scarlet; a few poplars and beeches yellowed the edge of the little lake, but most of the trees were green

green. We had had a muggy summer, but that day was worth waiting for through a month of muggy summers.

We were the only people at the lake. The park had closed officially on Labor Day. There was a small sign, Swim at Your Own Risk, but the whole place said Welcome.

That was one day I did not say, "Be careful," or, "Not too far out," or, "Stop that arguing." I cannot remember many such outings.

The bathhouses were two big rooms made of logs, open to the blue sky, with high window-squares to be looked through only if you stood on a bench. "Gee, it's like a fort," Mark said. "I forgot it was like a fort."

The boys were into their trunks in seconds. They were already in the water before I got my trousers off. Standing on the bench I watched the boys through one of the square portholes.

It is a pleasure for a man to watch his sons.

Charlotte appeared at the door. She wore the ruffled pants Mother had made. "Mama is a-stuck."

"Charlotte," Anna called from her fort.

"She's in here, in the men's room." Back then it was funny for Charlotte to be in the men's room.

"Well, bring her in here and help me with this darned zipper."

In the ladies' room I swung Charlotte to my shoulders. Anna and I kissed. Charlotte patted our heads.

Anna said, only half mocking, "Charlotte is an angel, blessing her parents."

Charlotte sang, "Schawl-ut is a angel, angel, angel." She waved her arms over her head. "Schawl-ut is a nangel, skippety mum per lou."

"You know what the last one in is," the boys called, as they had always called. They stood on the stationary platform in the middle of the swimming area. Each held to the ladder of the high diving board.

"How's the water?" we asked, as we had always asked.

"The water's fine."

173

Charlotte ran screaming into two inches of water, and out, and in again.

"Let's see a dive," Anna called.

Archer said, "You go first, Mark. It's your birthday."

Mark said, "Maybe I'll do it right this time, but you go first. You show me."

Oh, I am poorly put together. I was always touched when the boys were gentle with each other. I didn't look at Anna.

Archer dived, not a spectacular dive, but an adequate one. We applauded. Mark said, "That was pretty neat. Better'n all right."

Archer did everything better than all right: tennis, carpentry, his schoolwork. Only on rare occasions was he struck with a passion—his leaf collection won first prize at the state fair in Louisville; when he was fourteen his history of Graham County, written because he wanted to write it, was published as a pamphlet by the State Historical Society. Archer moved gracefully through being young.

Mark's enthusiasms embraced the world. He excelled in enthusiasm. He was never so efficient as Archer, but he did everything with passion. He worked hard and with joy; I can't remember his ever expressing disappointment over any failure. He was particularly poor at diving.

We watched Mark dive five or six times—fall, rather, to belly flop, to try again, his stomach as red as a lobster. "Was that better? Was that a little better? Here I go again. Watch. Watch now."

"Okay. Let's see you," Anna called.

Charlotte stopped being a sandpiper to look at Mark.

The boy stood on his toes, raised his hands, smiled at us, breathed deeply, and soared.

Mark floated in the air, gold-colored against the blue, against green, knifing into the water, his body as straight as an exclamation point.

I held my breath as if I, too, had flown, as if I were underwater, pushing toward the sun.

Mark appeared from far out in the water, beyond the buoys that marked the swimming area. He began to swim, clumsily, back to the platform.

174

Charlotte squealed.

Archer said, "Gol-lee."

Anna held her hands over her mouth. There were tears in her eyes. "My. Lovely," Anna said against her hands.

Mark, awkward, climbed on to the platform. Archer slapped him on the back. We shouted our congratulations. Charlotte sang, "Markie is a bir-ud, skiptum skiptum dee."

"I did it, didn't I?" Mark was shivering.

"Like the Olympics," Anna called.

Mark was embarrassed. "You all shut up."

That day was one of those rare days when time shows off, when it performs all the tricks it is capable of. It lingered. We swam, we lay in the sun. Charlotte slept. "We should eat, shouldn't we?" Anna and I asked each other every once in a while. The sun stood high in the sky.

"They're having such fun."

Again and again Mark dived. He was never to move so exquisitely as he had moved that long floating minute; but Mark had learned to dive.

Time had raced.

Archer and Mark stood over us. "I'm hungry," Mark said. "My stomach's stuck to my backbone."

"Yeah. When are we going to eat?"

As I walked toward the car I realized I had failed to bring the food—the thermoses, the sandwiches, the cake—from the kitchen table.

Anna said, "You couldn't have forgot."

"Wow! A birthday dinner without any food."

Mark began to laugh. He rolled in the sand laughing.

They were not cross with me. We gathered our gear and raced home. We had our picnic on the back porch. It must have been four-thirty or five when we ate.

That day was a good day to happen to a boy on his twelfth birthday: a perfect dive, watched by all of his family.

Anna has stopped reading what I am writing.

I have been writing for Anna. I have thought I was writing for Anna.

I have promised to keep on writing.

The sun feels good on my back.

Day before yesterday I had just finished writing about Mark's birthday when Anna came home for lunch. She said The Girls didn't feel up to a little drive, but they had insisted that we have an outing of our own. "Wasn't that nice of them? How did the writing go?"

"So-so. I've written about Mark's twelfth birthday. You can read it now if you want to."

Anna began busying herself in the kitchen. "We must keep to the schedule." She sounded exactly like Aunt Gloria. Anna can be a devastating mimic when she chooses to be. "I've been thinking about Mark, too."

"He was a fine boy."

"We have some Christmas shopping to do."

"I thought you'd brought everything from Graham. I thought everything was wrapped and ribboned."

"There's Junior. And Darling. I'd like to get a little something for the New Zealand boys. You don't have anything for me, do you? I don't have anything for you. We need to get some no-surprises for each other. We didn't mean it when we said we weren't going to get each other anything. Did we? You were going to cheat, weren't you? You planned on going out to buy me something.''

I admitted that I had planned to cheat.

"I'm glad. I'm glad you don't have a lot of character.''

The afternoon was warm enough for only a jacket.

We went through Nieman-Marcus and Saks and Bergdorf Goodman, rich stores where most of the customers looked as affluent as the Christmas decorations. We watched the skaters at the Galleria. We had tea and little sandwiches at a tea shoppe where the waitresses were dressed like page boys and shepherdesses.

I kept saying, "Just think. This goes on all the time.''

Anna said, "It's strange to think about, isn't it? And Skyview and Bonita Avenue are going on at the same time. We should buy a book about Houston.''

Anna said, "It's easier here than at home, isn't it? You're enjoying this, aren't you?''

I did not need to ask what she meant.

Sometimes at Christmases in Graham, walking through a K mart or the Super Warehouse, I have been almost overcome with melancholy at the children and the women and the men who fumble in their purses, their pockets, recount their change, fearful of having to return one of the glittering objects they have selected for someone they had hoped to surprise or bless.

It has been a long time since I was such a person, forced to leave the sled or the doll or the silver earrings on the counter, making trouble for the checkout girl, apologizing to the manager.

Anna's right. I'm no better shopper than I am traveler.

She's right when she says I have a depression mind. But she is not unsympathetic. Even before we left Graham she began saying, "No surprises for each other this Christmas. We must make everything easy for ourselves.''

It is difficult to bear the kindness of gifts at home, among walls you are long familiar with: the expectant look of the givers as they wait for you to remove the ribbon and paper, to say, "I've always wanted . . .''

177

When he was ten Mark gave me a milkstool he had made in Woodwork, a splintered circle of board on three legs that refused to hold the circle.

"What I've always wanted," I said, placing my coffee cup on the stool, which tipped over, spilling my coffee on to Archer's gift to me, two Audubon prints from The Bookstore, turning the robin into a blackbird, the nuthatch into a Rorschach test.

Archer was livid. "Look what you did. You've ruined Christmas."

Mark grabbed a wad of tissue paper and began rubbing the birds, upsetting his cocoa.

I have not thought of the milkstool Christmas for a long time. If Anna were going to be reading these pages tonight, I would not be remembering now.

At Nieman-Marcus we bought a Snoopy pillow for Junior, a scarf for Darling, a game for the little New Zealand boys; at Saks, for each other we bought a sweater and four paperback books; at Bergdorf, gloves for Anna, a sturdy key case for me—I keep being afraid I will lose the keys to 181 Bonita, a thought not to be borne. We went back to Nieman Marcus to buy an eighteen-inch glass tree with a light bulb in its base—as lovely, Anna said, as a window from Chartres. The gifts were generously expensive. We rather relished our extravagances. It was comforting not to see one human being count out his change. Anna said she felt very rich just walking through the stores.

We desposited our purchases at Skyview and rushed to The Girls'. We had missed Trixie's visit. Trixie had sent us many loving messages. She had left The Girls two identical boxes, beautifully wrapped. Poor Trixie. She was going to Dallas to spend the holiday with a cousin-in-law, somebody named Pauline whom she didn't really care much for. "Oh, yes," Aunt Gloria said, "she brought you all a present, too. It's in the kitchen. I put water in it. She said it wasn't for Christmas, but just for instance. That Trixie. We gave her a letter opener. She called to say she was coming over. I had it wrapped up before she got here."

Trixie had brought us a crystal vase of pink and white carnations. Anna and I were properly overcome. Perhaps we were too complimentary.

Mother said, "Carnations are not my flower. I prefer sweet peas. And lilacs."

Aunt Gloria said, "Carnations are for funerals. I thought we had discussed the matter of flowers with Trixie. Be sure you put a coaster under that vase, Anna."

I have put off writing about night before last.

I had thought Anna was pleased with what I was writing. At some few passages she has almost cried. Sometimes she has laughed. She has said, "I can't wait to find out what happens to us next." Once she said, "People will write articles about you and Archer. He's stolen your name, but you can be Lee Baxter. That sounds more like an author anyhow."

Once she said, "You're saving time."

It has been pleasant to hear Anna read. I have lain on my couch, my arms under my head, and studied the ceiling. The words sound better in Anna's voice than in mine.

When we got back here to Skyview, Anna was slow at settling down to read.

Several times she stopped reading, but I had no notion she was upset. I smiled at the ceiling, pleased with Anna's voice, remembering that September day without grief.

When she had finished, we were quiet for a minute. Then I said, "That was a great dive."

Anna said, "It's not a good idea, Arch."

I was slow in hearing her. Sometimes at home the mantel clock strikes and I do not hear it until after the sound stops. But I am always able to reconstruct the time, remembering the sounds I have not listened to.

"What's not a good idea?"

"Reading this way. I'm not going to read any more."

I sat up quickly. "What's the matter with you?"

Anna was looking at me as if I were somebody she had not met for a long time. She herself was looking like her passport picture. I wondered idly what photographers thought about the passport pictures they produced. "I'm just not going to read any more. It isn't fair to you. Or me either."

"What are you talking about, for God's sake. It's all your idea."

"I know. And you mustn't stop. I'd die if you stopped."

"What in the hell!"

"You're making us all different. I can't stand it." Anna spoke quietly. "I don't need to stand it. Not here. Not in Houston."

I was across the room. Anna stood. I was holding her shoulders. "What the hell, Anna? Listen to me. Look at me." I was shaking her shoulders.

"Let go of me. Get your hands off me."

Anna's bones were hard in my hands.

"You're hurting me, Arch. Stop it." Anna was shouting.

I loosened my hands.

Anna slapped me. The sound of her hand on my cheek was loud in the room.

I feel sure she was surprised, as I was. She lifted her hand again. She patted my cheek. Three times she patted my cheek.

She backed away from me. She backed clear to the wall behind the dinette table.

Two roaches moved on the wall above her head. I grabbed the manuscript from the table. I slashed at the roaches. I beat at the wall after the roaches fell to the floor. The face of the passport woman did not move.

I took the pages, the last page smeared with the bodies of the roaches, to the scarlet garbage can. I lifted the lid carefully. I did not have the energy to crumple the pages. I dropped them on to the apple peels and orange rinds and coffee grounds. My hands were trembling. They looked like Aunt Gloria's hands.

Anna ran her tongue over her lips, as if she had to prime them to speak. "I was furious with you for forgetting to pack the lunch."

"No, you weren't."

"I'd worked hard. I was having my period. The Girls had just left. That was the summer they stayed three months. I wanted to have a party Mark wouldn't forget. He did have. I was silly."

"He didn't have time to forget it." I suppose I wanted to hurt Anna. I was hurting myself. "Even if it had been a bad day."

"That night you went to sleep the minute you hit the bed. I wanted to talk about the dive. I knew he was going to die. You make fun of my feelings, but I had a notion he was going to die."

"Come off it, Anna."

"That night . . . I thought maybe we could get ready for it. Talk about it. It was a terrible night, Arch."

"My God."

"I loved Mark more than the others. I know it's terrible to say. I used to think God would punish me. But I haven't been punished, not really. I have a feeling I won't be now, at least not for loving Mark too much."

I held to the edge of the bar.

"I don't like the way you lie, Arch. You're making things pretty. That was his last birthday. All you remember is the dive. You'll make his funeral pretty. And the days after. You don't remember the way things really were."

"Goddamn it, Anna, I'm trying to write what I remember."

"It's like practicing death after it's all over. Don't you know what I mean?"

"I have no notion in God's world."

"You've got to write it, but I don't have to read it." Anna was moving toward me. "Some days I think you and I love each other too much. But I don't have any feelings about us, not any of those feelings."

Our arms were around each other. Anna dug her fingernails into my back.

"Anna, Anna."

Anna pulled away. "Your poor face." She patted my face. "I'm sorry."

I said, "I'm sorry." I imagined myself standing at the front door, watching the man and the woman. The man and woman had had a scene, a more violent scene than they had ever had in their married life. Still, it was a very small scene. I felt only drained. *Embalmed* is a better word.

Anna said, "I want to read it all sometime, all the way through."

I said, "Tomorrow's another day," echoing myself, and Mother, and the dim voice of my father.

Anna said, "We remember what we can remember. I didn't mean you don't remember."

I said, "You take your bath first."

Anna said, "I will, if you don't mind. I'm a touch weary, as Mil says."

I reached down to take the pages from the garbage can. My back creaked. Anna stood by the vanity counter, watching me.

I cleaned the pages as well as I was able, using three paper napkins from the red plastic napkin holder.

"Kiss me, Arch."

We kissed. Anna leaned hard against me. We were awkward.

I had been angry with Anna because she had hurt my pride.

I cannot believe I had been angry because she seemed to doubt my grief.

When a man pulls his vanity down, or it's pulled down for him, what does he stand on? Where does he stand?

I have grieved over Mark more than I had imagined a man could grieve.

After nineteen years I still dream of the boy. "See ya, Dad." "See ya, Mark." He bicycles down the hill.

It was months after his death before I realized I had spent a whole hour without thinking of him. I felt good. I told myself that grief, any grief, was a luxury, that Anna, Archer, Charlotte, and I must live.

After a while I believed what I kept telling myself.

I was living whole days without thinking of the boy.

After the first months Anna and I mentioned him less often. We never spoke of him where Archer and Charlotte could hear. "They are alive," I told and told myself. They were alive in a house which held most of what they would remember about being young, about their parents.

After a while, a year, Anna was herself again. She began taking courses at the college, finishing the degree she had given up to take care of her parents, to marry me, to bear children.

I assumed she had made what peace a human being is capable of making with a word like *grief*.

Perhaps we should have talked more together.

I do not know what we could have said.

As I remember, we stayed at Baldwin Lake until midafternoon. We laughed when we discovered that I had forgotten the picnic dinner.

At home, as I remember, when Anna began to set the table, Mark said, "This is supposed to be a picnic, Mom. Let's eat on the back porch. You aren't supposed to sit in chairs at a picnic."

As I remember, we sat on the beach towels spread on the concrete floor. We were ravenous. Mark's funny menu was delicious. We ate every crumb. Anna made more sandwiches. We had cocoa after the Cokes were gone. We all went to bed early.

I remember that Mark said, "I wish I could go on being twelve forever."

Perhaps he did not say that. But I am pretty sure he said, "I wish I could go on being twelve forever." Anyhow, he got his wish.

I did not write yesterday.

Perhaps I have incorrectly remembered what happened night before last.

Already I can't remember anything that happened yesterday. Except Anna said, "My, but I'm feeling good. I was terribly tired last night. I have a feeling, Arch. Everything's going to be fine."

I said, "Sure. Sure."

"We don't even have to think about last night. Is that all right with you?"

"Sure. Of course."

But I am not writing for Anna now, not for a long time.
Or I am writing for Anna.

Aunt Gloria has decided that we are to call her Gloria from now on.

Mother said, "Don't be kittenish, Gloria."

"I mean it, Donna Dale. I've waited all my life for Archie to get as old as I am. It came to me last night. We're all the same age now. I'm not one whit older than Archie and Anna. I am Gloria. G-L-O-R-I-A. Ain't we got fun!"

"Yes." I found it difficult to look at her. "Maybe I'm even older."

Mother said, "We are *not* the same age as the children. We should admit it."

"I'm not admitting it. That's what's so nice about a family. Eventually you all get to be the same age. Isn't that true, Arch?"

"I'm sure it's true, Aunt Gloria."

"Gloria, Gloria, Gloria! Say it three times after me. Somebody used to call me 'Glory' once upon a time. You can call me Glory if you want to." Aunt Gloria was actually blushing.

Mother said, "Gloria is quite sufficient."

Aunt Gloria said, "We're all old enough to be dead and buried."

"Gloria! The very idea!" Mother was aghast.

"I was funning. I was just funning, Sister."

Some days I feel no older than twelve.

How much of being young does a man, a couple, carry over into being old?

Somebody, Archer maybe, could write a little play or a story on the subject.

He would need to start the story in the past, 1947, say, in August, the day before a wedding anniversary.

This is a story. I am writing a story.

The man locked his mother's suitcases in the trunk of the 1939 Chevrolet coupe. The coupe had belonged to the man's wife. She had bought the car when she was being a social worker for the county. She often reminded her husband: "That Chevy is my dowry. Don't think you married somebody without a dowry."

The man went back into the house, closing the screen door carefully, the way he had been taught to close screen doors. His mother and his wife stood in the center of the little living room.

"One more look," the mother said.

"Oh Mil." The man knew his wife was going to cry.

"Please, Mother."

The man's mother was apologizing again for leaving the couple on the day before their second wedding anniversary. "I hate to leave on such an important occasion, but it suits Sister better for me to arrive on the weekend. I so wanted to take you to Winchester and the Old South Inn for dinner, a very fine dinner." Her voice was as bright as if she were welcoming a state meeting of the Women's Club to Graham College.

"Oh, my. We'll miss you." The wife was crying.

"Here, none of that. I'll be back in a month or two, as soon as Sister recuperates."

The aunt was having a hysterectomy. In that household, illnesses were rarely named, much less discussed. The mother referred to her sister's illness, when she referred to it at all, as "female trouble."

The mother put her arms around the daughter-in-law, holding her tightly. "You're my blessed Dilly. And there's a little something in that envelope behind the clock. You aren't to open it until tomorrow. You hear?"

Ever since the three of them had moved into the old house on Oak Street, the mother had insisted that she contribute fifty dollars to the household budget. The money came from her husband's insurance check of ninety-seven fifty. "Where else could I live so well? Hush, silly," she said a hundred times. "This is your mother speaking."

The man reached for the envelope tucked behind the Seth Thomas clock. "No, Mother."

He saw himself in the gilt-framed mirror, reaching for the envelope, a real envelope that reflected itself behind the clock. In the mirror the face of the envelope showed their names, his wife's and his, reversed. He knew that the envelope said, "With love overflowing, Mother."

"No, Mother. Really no." He was determined. "You didn't even let us buy your train ticket. You're being impossible."

"Put that back." Her voice was cold. "Son, put that back."

"Please, Mother." The man was almost shouting.

"You needn't shout." She released her daughter-in-law. "If I've tried to teach you anything . . ."

The man was angry. If she had tried to teach him anything, it was that ladies and gentlemen never lifted their voices, did not discuss monetary matters or any matters of the flesh, did not wash their dirty linen in public. At dusk ladies and gentlemen lowered their blinds as well as their voices, considering the neighbors.

187

The man was six inches taller than his mother, but that day they looked at each other on the same level. Perhaps the mother stood on tiptoe; perhaps the man slouched. The man felt as if he were looking into a mirror. He supposed he should have felt comforted, have experienced a sense of shared vision, but he did not so feel. He was disturbed by the mirror of his mother's eyes.

Almost thirty-five years later, leaning down to speak to his mother in her chair, he would remember the moment in front of the mantel when he and his mother had looked at each other exactly.

The young man was given to rather sententious thoughts. He thought, "Perhaps all mirrors lie, even the mirror of love itself." He replaced the envelope behind the clock.

"Sweetheart. Baby. Come on now. Don't sull." The mother placed her white gloves and navy blue purse on the mantel. She straightened her hat.

The hat was new, navy-blue straw with a white band and three white daisies, paid for out of her monthly forty-seven dollars and fifty cents. Her suit and white blouse, an outfit she had bought for her son's graduation from college, was still handsome.

The son said, "You look handsome."

"Doesn't she, though? Just beautiful."

After two years of marriage the son was almost always able to tell when his wife was going to cry. He did not need to look at her to tell. The couple was sympathetic.

"Darn you. I'm not going to cry any more," the wife said, crying.

"What kind of farewell is this? Come on, the both of you. You know how I hate to be late."

"Donna Dale wants to get to the station at least a day ahead of time." That was a family saying, inherited from somebody.

"Exactly." The mother turned in a circle, looking at the objects in the couple's living room, in *her* living room, really, the couch, the coffee table, the drapes, even the wallpaper. The mother had chosen the wallpaper after the three of them moved into the house.

The mother had not imposed her tastes on the daughter-in-law. The daughter-in-law—we will call her Anna for convenience' sake—said, "You have a way with a house, Mil. Please—you

choose." The mother had even suggested the silver and china patterns. "Please—you choose."

The mother stood holding open the screen door. The man
thought, surprised at his lack of charity, "But, by God, we paid for
the wallpaper," surprised at his thinking *by God*.

He wished he and Anna were rich. He wished he were driving his
mother to the airport in Lexington. He imagined a first class seat for
her, a taxi to take her across Houston to his aunt's place. He
thought, "Goddamn it." He said, "We'll miss you. We love you. I
love you."

"Of course you do." The older woman was not going to cry.
"We all love each other very much. Come on. Tracks. Make tracks,
everybody."

Anna hiccoughed.

They were forty minutes early. The train was a half hour late.

They sat in the hot station under a ceiling fan that turned sleepily.
They made talk. The mother remembered two library books she had
forgotten to return. She said she didn't know what had happened to
her mind. Anna said, "I'll trade you any day."

The mother said that the young couple must write. "Once a
week? Is once a week too much?"

Anna said she would probably be boring the mother with her
letters, with questions—what to do with the tomato plants, for
instance.

The mother said the tomatoes were more Anna's than anybody's.
"Who did the weeding?"

Anna asked who did the planning and the planting and the
suckering.

The son said they should have called the station to check before
they left home.

Mother smiled. "I'm afraid none of us is that kind of person."

The women laughed together.

The son went to ask Mr. Sawyer, who sat in his stationmaster's
cage, if he had heard anything more. Mr. Sawyer said he didn't
know what had got into Old Two-Twenty.

189

"That fan, honestly," Anna was saying. "You can count each
blade as it goes by. We could *name* them."

"Tom, Dick, Harry, and who else?" Mother said.

"How do you like George?"

George was just fine with Mother—we will refer to her as Mother for convenience' sake. The women were totally companionable. The son envied their camaraderie.

He went to the restroom. He read the signs on the walls. He splashed cold water on his face. He combed his hair carefully. He imagined he heard a train's whistle. He hurried from the room.

"Now it's my turn," Mother said. "Here. Take care of my purse and gloves."

"She's a dear," Anna said. "We're going to miss her."

"I thought I heard a whistle. She mustn't stay in there too long. If she misses the train . . ." The son imagined the train's barely pausing at the station. He imagined the engineer's ignoring their calls, Mr. Sawyer's hoarse shout.

Ignominiously the three people would return to their home. There would be telephone calls, unpacking, the long evening and the long morning, the trip to the station again. If the son's mother had not gone to the restroom, the man and his wife would be alone in their house for the first time in their married lives. They would be alone together.

"There," Mother said, settling herself. "All fat and cozy and smelling sweet." Anna laughed. She knew the family sayings as well as the Baxters knew them. A long time ago some child in Millersburg had said the words first, perhaps before the young man had been born.

He wondered if his wife and he would have time enough together to collect sayings of their own.

"Now, you aren't to worry about us. I'll call if I need you. Sister's health is basically very good. She's strong."

How many times had they gone over the details, as if talk would save them all. "Gloria needs me. She'd do the same for me. I figure on a month until she gets really well."

The train was there. A porter placed a metal stepstool for Mother to mount the train. She was the only person leaving Graham that still August day.

This is not a story at all. I am incapable of making up a story.

"Hurry, hurry," I said, but not aloud.

I lifted Mother's bags to the conductor in the vestibule. "Now you take care of yourselves." Mother was hugging and kissing Anna, making the train wait. Mother and I embraced. We kissed on either cheek. Mother smelled of lilacs, like her handkerchief drawer, like her closet.

"Hurry home. Hurry back," Anna said brokenly. "Love to Aunt Gloria."

At a window Mother tapped her handkerchief of Florentine lace. It was her best handkerchief—Cousin Lil had brought it to her twenty years ago. Mother gestured to us, some message, her lips moved. I couldn't imagine what she was saying. I lifted my shoulders. Anna nodded as if she understood.

We threw kisses at each other.

"All uh-*boart!*" the conductor called, and the train groaned away. I did not look at Anna. My throat was full of her tears.

We waved to the train until it disappeared a half mile down the track, at the bend of Dead Man's Curve.

I wondered if I would ever see her again, as I regularly and ridiculously wonder when people I love, or merely like, move from my spot of earth in airports, stations, even in front of our house, to far places. I have known the same bereavement and loss when the family car or a bicycle bears someone away, if only to town or school.

Always my anxieties have been unfounded. Almost always. Yes, always. I am given to premonitions, but without any reason.

I honestly did not think I would never see Mark again when he jumped on his bicycle that morning, almost late for school, as usual, when he called to me, when I called to him.

I picked up the newspaper from the top of the privet hedge. The delivery boy that fall was a very poor marksman.

I had no intimation of what Police Chief Quigley was going to say into the telephone when he called twenty minutes later.

Blessedly, I have failed as clairvoyant.

When something especially good happens to us, Anna always says, "Gloomy Arch has just failed his fortune-telling course again." It is one of our family sayings.

But I am not gloomy; I do not consider myself gloomy.

"Gloom is a wickedness," Mother has always said. "Things work together." I have tried to believe her.

She was not to live with us again. The semiannual visits have been a kind of living with us. Things work out. I am grateful that she has not lived with us permanently. I am blessed.

That afternoon, when Mother's train left a hole in the landscape, Anna said, "Your handkerchief. I'm all out of Kleenexes."

I said, "Anna, Anna."

She did not stop dabbing at her eyes the whole two miles of our trip home. In the driveway she said, "Wait a minute. I'm all right. I don't want Mrs. Scheible to see me carrying on." She blew her nose vigorously. I patted her knee.

"What was it your grandmother used to say about seeing people off, Miss Anna?"

"I know, I know. I was thinking about it. But Mil's so nice. A person can cry a little extra for her."

Anna's grandmother used to say, "Weep as much as you please over partings, but stop when the ship's out of sight."

We walked across the front yard and into our house.

I was pleased to have thought of the grandmother quote, feeling close to an old woman I had never seen, as if Anna's family were also mine. It was a comfortable feeling that day, although there have been seasons when I have wished that our forebears had been mutes.

I said, "August weather. Tomato weather can be finer than June roses."

I hope I did not say, "There's no place like home," as I hung the car keys on the hook in the coat closet. I thought, but surely I did not say, "A place for everything and everything in its place." The key hooks had been Mother's idea, with quotation attached.

I was excited.

"Aren't you going back to the store? Isn't Mr. McKelvy expecting you?"

"No. No, I have time coming to me. He said it was all right."

Anna walked through the living room and into the dining room. At the kitchen door she turned. She was smiling. "Arch, I'm embarrassed. I'm embarrassed to be alone with you."

I like to think we both hurried to each other. We were kissing as we had never kissed in the light of day. We were laughing as we had never laughed in our bedroom upstairs whose wall did not really separate us from Mother's bed. Although Anna and I, and Mother, pretended we were distant neighbors at night, we failed at our pretense.

"I'm sorry you didn't sleep well last night, Mil," Anna would say at breakfast, in spite of herself.

"I don't like those coughs. You ought to let Dr. Thompson have a look at the both of you," Mother said.

Making love was a dark secret, more often on the floor than on the bed, often not at all. But that August day we were noisy. I locked the front and back doors noisily. We walked upstairs, our arms around each other.

I said, "We'll go in here," pulling Anna into Mother's room.

"Really? Not really, Arch." But she did not hold back.

If I had said, "Let's fuck on Mother's bed," if I had dared offend Anna, myself, our language, our rearing, our proprieties . . . if I had dared, perhaps our marriage would have taken a different turn; perhaps we would have been as free as Charlotte and Archer seem to be, unworried about words like *responsibility* or *the generations*. I rather gather that freed language reflects freed minds, even bodies.

Or perhaps Anna and I could not have happened in other words.

But I did say, "We'll go in here," and Anna did not hold back.

We made love noisily on Mother's bed, on the lavender counterpane. I did not wonder if Mother's train had broken down just past Dead Man's Curve, if a kind stranger had brought her home, if she were opening the front door with the key she kept pinned to the lining of her purse, or if she were mounting the steps to discover us, to cry out her betrayal.

Her betrayal in what?

194

I know only that she would have felt betrayed.

We were noisy and abandoned. We had sex. We made love. That day and night, unretouched, have been the stuff of my fantasies through sets of years.

Afterward we lay quiet.

Afterward I imagined Mother's returning from the broken train, standing at her bedroom door, catching us.

It was Anna who whispered, "Let's go in our room. Where we can talk."

I carried her into our room. Together we fell onto our bed.

"Arch. Lovely Arch." We pulled back the covers together. "Cozy," Anna said against my ear. She cleared her throat. In an almost normal voice she said, "Isn't this cozy, though?"

We were laughing. The sheets smelled of sun. The net curtains at the windows lifted and fell and lifted. Billows. They were the meaning of billows. The leaves of the sycamore moved outside; they said and resaid their shadows against the ceiling.

"It's marvelous, isn't it?" I did not say, "having her gone."

"Wonderful."

Perhaps the language of lovers is always foolish.